BATHHOUSE

CONFESSIONS

2

NATHAN BAY

First edition: July 2019

Bay Cove Press

ISBN: 9781076783257

CONTENTS

FOG CITY

TEMPTATION

CHAPTER 1

San Francisco - June, 1955

The summer fog was snaking through the city, swallowing up the land below. I watched as purple skies disappeared from the horizon, blotted out by glittery grey plumes.

This was my favorite time of day, when my work was done and I finally had the opportunity to sit down and enjoy the view from the Sea Cliff mansion I called home.

I sipped from my glass of tea, tasting the tangy fresh peach infusion bubbling on my tongue. The flavor reminded me of my childhood, when my mother always had a fresh pitcher sitting on the porch. You'd never find a sunset like this back in Kansas.

Nobody would aspire to have my life, but I was quite content with it. From six in the morning until four in the afternoon, I was a fisherman. Five days a week and sometimes weekends too.

My main trade was in Dungeness crab. That was the real money-maker. When crab wasn't in season, I would go out looking for fish. That didn't pay as well as crab, but it kept me busy and it was nice to always have money in my pocket.

My employer was Mr. Frank Ritts. He and his wife Rita were big-time dealers with the local markets. They were good people who handled the business end while I did the dirty work at sea.

I didn't mind. Mr. and Mrs. Ritts had taken good care of me for the past few years. In addition to the salary I was paid, they'd also given me free board in their cozy little guesthouse. It wasn't a bad arrangement for a twenty-five-year-old like me who hadn't even gone to college.

The view to my right was the magnificent Golden Gate Bridge, standing high above the clouds in all her deep orange-colored glory. Straight ahead of me was miles and miles of endless blue ocean, as far and wide as the eyes could see. And just below, to my left, a paved path led down the sandy hillside to China Beach, a quiet little spot where I liked to go for long walks.

After finishing my drink, I changed out of my bathrobe into a neatly pressed pair of grey tweed slacks and a white button-up shirt. Evenings were bitingly cold by the bay, even during the summertime, so I slid on my long black wool overcoat. I felt like something was missing so I topped my blond hair with a matching fedora and tucked a red feather in the ribbon.

I was a bit overdressed, but I enjoyed looking nice in my personal time since I was often covered in fish guts and sea sludge during the daytime.

The nights belonged to me, and since it was Friday, that meant I'd be making my weekly trip to a little place called The Pacific Health Club & Spa for Men. The name was a mouthful to say, much less remember. Men who were 'in the know' simply called it The Pacific. It was a mile walk south, past the affluent homes of Sea Cliff and over to the bustling strips of restaurants and shops on Geary Boulevard.

The Pacific was a bathhouse, but on the record, it was touted as a private gymnasium for men. It was the only gym I'd ever seen that barricaded its windows with heavy drapes. A small, almost invisible black placard sign on the front door was the only indicator of the name.

Every step of my twenty-minute stroll to the 'gym' seemed to amplify the tingling of my sensitive cock as it rubbed against the soft cotton of my boxer shorts. It had been a week since I'd last shot my load and I felt like a shaken bottle of champagne ready to be uncorked. I liked to let my anticipation build so my one night of splendor would be extra special.

When I arrived at the bathhouse, I greeted Jimmy, the owner, on the way in the front door and dropped two quarters on the counter. He tried to slide them back to me but I insisted on paying. After all, I wanted to help support his business so he could keep it open.

Jimmy never wanted me to pay for admission, but I felt it was only fair. I was a working man, just like any other, and I wasn't looking for any hand-outs. He liked to say that waiving my entrance fee was his way of giving thanks for my help on sprucing up the place. But I enjoyed helping him make it nicer. He was always open to my suggestions.

Past the linoleum-floored foyer was a small room with your basic equipment: a bench for lifting weights, a worn and torn punching bag that looked like it had finally given up the fight, and a few jump ropes that were unraveling at the seams. In the two years that I'd been visiting The Pacific, I'd never once seen a man using the makeshift gym. It was beyond the main entryway and around the corner where the magic really happened.

There was a large hall of open showers, ten heads on each side, lined in turquoise blue ceramic tiles. The tile was new, installed that past spring. I'd helped Jimmy pick out the tile color when he replaced the old, cracked white ones.

I greeted some familiar faces as I made my way to the locker area and undressed for the showers. It would be my third time bathing that day. I'd showered once in the morning after my jog, then again after work to prepare for my night out. That one was my deep cleanse, where I made sure everything was up to code. My third shower, the one I took at The Pacific, was merely for entertainment. Soaping up and standing naked under the water was part of a social ritual. *Peacocking*, as I once heard someone call it. Besides, good hygiene was really important to me.

Speaking of birds who liked to show off, the cock of the walk was making himself known as he strutted into the showers. Brown-haired, blue-eyed Leonard Sutton. We called him Lenny.

Lenny was a handsome fella, kind of full of himself, but he kept the place interesting with his boisterous attitude. He also enjoyed a good prank.

If somebody was new, he'd initiate them by chucking their clothes into the jacuzzi. Sometimes he'd snatch their garments and hide the pile in someone else's locker. That was a trick he liked to play on shy guys who seemed quiet or nervous. Lenny claimed it was good for morale because it forced his unsuspecting victims to go around chatting with other men as they searched for their clothes. *A stranger is just a friend you haven't met yet.*

Lenny grabbed a clean towel, twirled it and then let it snap against my bottom. He always greeted me that way. It didn't hurt, but I always feigned surprise. We both laughed as he wrapped his arms around me in a friendly embrace. Our naked bodies pressed together and he made a show of rubbing our cocks together.

I greeted him with a kiss on the cheek. "Hey there, Lenny, good to see you."

"Good to be seen, Charles," he said, sniffing a little at my neck. "How's it hanging tonight?"

"You tell me."

Lenny took my hardening cock into his hand and gave it a firm squeeze. "Not bad at all."

That was as far as it would go and I knew it. He bit his lower lip and made a gruff sound that reminded me of a bulldog in heat before taking a spot at the shower across from me.

We'd always had a strange, playful energy between us that never moved on to the next level. I sometimes thought that Lenny got more enjoyment out of flirting and rubbing up against guys than he did from actual sex. It was rare that I heard about or saw him make a connection with someone else.

There were a lot of psychological barriers when it came to sex with other men. Lenny's style of touchy, grabby stuff could be written off as general banter that was common in the bathhouse. Being alone with someone in a private room required a little more vulnerability.

I took my time soaping up my long and lean body as the water washed over me. I wasn't stacked but I kept in good shape. My arms were toned, my abs were tight. My chest was firm and mostly smooth except for a tangle of curls in the middle of my pecs.

Most of the other guys in the showers were regulars; several I'd had some flings with. We greeted each other with knowing nods.

When I was finished rinsing off, I grabbed a towel and secured it around my waist, then headed out to enjoy the evening. Lenny was right behind me, drying off and walking toward the doors that led out back.

Past the showers was an open-air deck with a heated jacuzzi and plenty of seating. Ivy-wrapped trellises surrounded the parameter for added privacy and three fire pits provided a warm, cozy atmosphere.

Lenny chucked off his towel and dunked himself into the hot tub, sending waves that splattered other men who were trying to enjoy conversations. Lenny was oblivious to his disruption.

I had a more subtle approach. After casually flashing open my towel and draping it along the edge of the tub, I slowly lowered myself into the bubbly water, pretending to be adjusting to the warmth.

"Hey, Charles, don't be a wimp," Lenny said, flicking water into my face. "It's not that hot."

"Thanks for that observation," I commented dryly. While the water wasn't too hot, I was boiling over with sexual energy and Lenny was cramping my style.

"You see anything on the menu that looks good tonight?" he asked.

I surveyed the men standing around on the patio chatting in their white cotton uniforms. That's when a handsome stranger caught my eye.

He'd just strutted out the door alone. Quiet, confident, assessing his surroundings like a stealth spy. He had dark skin and black hair that was cut tight in a buzzcut. A silver set of dog tags hung from his neck. "Maybe that guy," I said, giving a nod in the stranger's direction.

Lenny giggled louder than he should have at an answer that wasn't even supposed to be funny. It was all part of his nervous exuberance.

The stranger took notice and turned his steely gaze right toward us with curiosity. The flickering light from the fire pit illuminated the soft brown in his eyes.

"Be cool," I whispered through clenched teeth, locked in a smile hoping the stranger wouldn't know we were talking about him.

Lenny turned his back to the guy and whispered to me, "He's really cute. Why do you think he has that necklace on?"

"Those are dog tags. He must be in the military."

"Ooh, a soldier. I wonder what kind of weaponry he's packing under that towel." Lenny hopped out of the tub and began to dry off. The soldier was eyeing us both, probably wondering what was going on as Lenny strolled over to him.

"Lenny, what are you doing?" I whispered.

But I was too late. Lenny was off on his mission.

He flashed a goofy smile at the soldier and the soldier smiled back awkwardly.

I knew something embarrassing was about to happen and all I could do was watch as it unfolded.

With the flick of his wrist, Lenny swiped the towel from the soldier's waist and ran inside, leaving the poor fella standing there naked and exposed in the middle of the patio. A group of men standing nearby snickered as the soldier clutched his jewels to maintain what little modesty he had left.

He took off after Lenny with an angry scowl on his face. At that moment I knew my friend had finally picked the wrong person to prank.

I grabbed my towel and darted after them, hoping to save Lenny from getting popped in the kisser. I tailed the soldier down the hallway over to the changing area just as he'd caught up to Lenny and cornered him against a row of lockers.

The soldier's voice boomed, "What the hell's the matter with you?" He snapped his towel back from Lenny's hands and wound up his fist.

"Wait a minute!" I called out, trying to wedge myself between them. "Lenny was just messing around with you."

The soldier sneered. "Messing with me will earn you a knuckle sandwich."

"I'm really sorry," Lenny said shakily.

"Let's just go somewhere and talk," I said, wrapping my arm around the soldier's shoulders. His skin was hot and inflamed with bulging veins.

He gave me a sidelong glance, and I thought maybe it was a mistake to touch him, but surprisingly he nodded. "Fine. Lead the way."

I took him down the hall to the furthest room at the end. It was a 'recovery suite,' as Jimmy called it. Because The Pacific was technically a health club, he couldn't refer to the suites as bedrooms.

The soldier sat down on the full-sized bed, trying to get comfortable on the thin mattress that was worn down to the springs. His chest was still heaving, but he seemed a little calmer, or at least less likely to murder someone. "Alright, I'm here. What do you want to say?"

I peeked out at the hallway where Lenny watched with a mixed expression of concern and curiosity. It was clear he was pretty rattled by being chased down.

"Are we talking or not?" the soldier grumbled.

"Yes." I closed the door behind me and turned the lock into place.

CHAPTER 2

Walking over to the side of the bed, I appraised the way the soldier's tight body curved with peaks and valleys. "What's your name, anyway?"

He studied me with skepticism. "Ricky."

"Ricky, my name's Charles. I think you got off to a bad start with Lenny and me."

"Why am *I* the one who got off to a bad start?" Ricky's jaw clenched tight. I was a little bit scared, but a little bit turned on too. He had such an alpha-male presence about him.

I held my hands up, trying to make peace. "Sorry, that came out wrong."

He forged on with his questioning. "Why were you and that knucklehead staring at me and laughing?"

"To be fair, Lenny was the only one laughing. I told him you were attractive."

The soldier raised an eyebrow. "And he thought it was funny that you found me attractive?"

I carried a rickety fold-up chair next to the bed and set it in place. My knee grazed against Ricky's skin, sending a tingle through my body. "No, it wasn't funny. Lenny was just goofing around. It's how he is. He laughs when he doesn't know what else to do with himself."

"Uh-huh."

I wasn't used to working so hard to convince a guy I liked him. "Why did you think Lenny was laughing at you?"

Ricky shot me a look as if the answer were obvious. "Because I'm a black man."

"Oh, I get the picture now." It hadn't occurred to me that he might think we were laughing at the color of his skin. The post-World War II era had brought many different ethnicities to San Francisco. I was so used to the diversity of the city, and the openness of the bathhouse, I hadn't considered what life must be like for a person of color. "Well look, Ricky, I can assure you we weren't making fun of you. Are you new to the area?"

"I've been here a few months," he said evenly.

"Okay. Well, maybe I could show you around sometime."

Ricky scoffed. "A lily white man like you walking around the streets with a dark-skinned guy like me? People would think I'm your chauffeur."

"That's not likely."

"Why not?"

"If anything," I explained, "people would think I'm *your* chauffeur. I make a living as a fisherman. That's not a job that usually comes with a chauffeur."

"People don't know you're a fisherman just by looking at you," Ricky said. "You can hide your job but I can't hide my skin color."

I cautiously put my hand on Ricky's knee. "You're making up assumptions. It's not like that here."

He pulled away. "I don't need you to tell me what it's like here or anywhere."

I nodded. "You're right." My skin is the color of porcelain with a swath of freckles that covers me like splattered paint. Aside from the occasional joke about how I look like a ghost, I'd never experienced true ridicule or discrimination for my skin tone. There was no comparison.

Ricky seemed to be tensing up again. His body looked stiff. He cracked his knuckles. I wasn't sure if that was a warning.

"Look, I've caused enough trouble for one night." I stood and dragged my chair back over to the wall. "Sorry again for any embarrassment Lenny and I caused you. We didn't mean anything by it. I just thought you were really handsome and hoped things might go differently. As far as Lenny grabbing the towel off you, I know that's not okay and I think he's learned his lesson. I'll chat with him about it just to make sure he understands."

As I turned toward the door, Ricky said, "Wait."

"Yes?"

A smile was pulling at the soldier's heart-shaped pillow lips. "You really think I'm handsome?"

"Hell, yes. I was lusting after you from the moment I laid eyes on you."

Ricky graced me with a dazzling grin that made me weak. His shoulders seemed to relax as he said, "You're pretty easy on the eyes too."

Maybe I had a chance with this sexy soldier after all. "Why don't I come over there to the bed and let you take a seat on my lap so I can enjoy the view?"

"Oh, so you want to fuck me?" he asked.

"I wouldn't be so brazen about it, but yeah, that's kinda the idea."

"Uh-huh." He tilted his head thoughtfully as if considering my offer. "Well, I have something else in mind."

I returned to his side and leaned in with a dopey grin painted across my face. "Oh, yeah?"

Just as I was about to sit down, he stood and slid past me. "Wait on the bed. I'll be right back."

Ricky opened the door to find Lenny leaned against the wood panel, trying to eavesdrop. The soldier pumped his chest and pretended to lunge for my nosy friend. Lenny squealed and took off running.

I snickered as I watched with anticipation, wondering what this mystery man was up to.

The soldier returned a minute later with a bundle of white rope wrapped around his hand. "During training, I was taught how to tie rope and knot it really well. I also had to learn how to escape from it."

"That's good to know," I said, unsure of where the conversation was going. It set afloat nervous butterflies in my stomach.

He continued, "And I've always had a sort of secret interest in it. There are things I've wanted to try with rope but never could."

"Such as?" I asked warily.

In the blink of an eye, he'd taken the rope and lassoed it around my nut sack in a loop, then tied another loop around my cock. His deft hands had me bound up nice and tight before I could even protest. The feeling was uncomfortably firm, but strangely, it didn't hurt.

"Hey, this isn't really my scene." I reached down to unbind my tautly-wrapped jewels but Ricky pushed my hand away.

"Leave it," he said.

"Or what?"

"Or I walk out of here."

I furrowed my brows and reluctantly sighed. "Fine."

"Fine, *sir*," he corrected."

I rebelled with a snort. "I'm not calling you that."

The soldier maintained his steely stare on me. "Call me sir or I leave." That delicious mouth of his was perpetually curled slightly upward, serving me an unspoken reminder that this was just a game. I couldn't decide whether I wanted to participate.

After a heavy silence, I finally conceded. "Alright, I'll play along, *sir*." My words were laced with sarcasm. "But if this starts to hurt, I'm tearing the rope off, got it?"

He snapped his fingers. "Don't you back talk me, boy! Get on your knees and polish my cock. *Now!*"

This time I responded with more obedience. "Yes, sir."

I knelt down on my knees and perched on the cold, rough concrete floor. My cock was turning dark red, bloated and stiff as marble. My nuts were protruding out, pulled together so uncomfortably tight. I reached between my legs to loosen the death grip of the rope but he shooed my hands away again.

"Didn't I tell you to leave it alone?"

"Yes, sir."

Ricky opened his towel to reveal the goods. His cock was long and thick, encased in a tight foreskin with bulging veins that roped around his shaft.

"You're not circumcised," I observed.

"Is that a problem?"

"Not at all, sir." Everything happened so fast outside, I hadn't noticed. I examined his cock as if it were an alien species. I'd never seen a foreskin up close. Seeing a natural penis preserved in all its glory was like a gift from the heavens.

"You want to play with it?"

I nodded with enthusiasm. But rather than skipping to the main course, I thought I'd start with the appetizer and address the two tennis balls stuffed in his scrotum. They were large and hung low against his thighs. I gently caressed them with the back of my hand. His body jolted at the sensation.

My touch was little more than a whisper. In my experience, men generally liked to go hard and rough. Being rough had its perks, but I'd found that going the opposite route could be even more intense. It was that cool, controlled touch that really drove them crazy. So I liked to take things slow and steady, just barely touching a man when he was craving full contact.

Ricky hovered over me with his hard cock throbbing and bobbing in the air. "What are you waiting for?" There was an edgy impatience in his voice.

"Just taking in the scenery," I coyly responded.

He grabbed the base of his hard cock and slapped it across my forehead. "Take it in faster."

Fuck. This soldier did not waste time. I was completely under his command. "Yes, sir," I said, gripping his cock.

"Why don't you see how it tastes?"

"Yes, sir."

His foreskin clung tight to his glans and bunched at the tip like a rosebud. I dipped my tongue inside and carefully pried it apart.

"Don't be afraid to get in there."

I responded by squeezing the root of his shaft and rolling his foreskin down to reveal a girthy bullet-shaped crown. It was dark pink and glistened like smooth glass. I swirled my tongue around the tip, then glided down his frenulum. He moaned softly, letting me know he enjoyed it, so I played with the thin band more before delving deeper into the underside.

The flavor inside the walls of his foreskin was a feast for the senses. Though he was fresh, clean, and clearly a beacon of good hygiene, there was a buttery zest that lingered on my tongue.

I swiped across his glans, hungrily lapping up a thick pearl of pre-cum that had leaked out.

"That's good, Charles," he praised, grabbing hold of my skull with both hands and driving me down on his cock.

My eyes watered and I thought I might choke. I couldn't breathe, but he kept pushing further. I relaxed my throat muscles and concentrated on breathing through my nose. With a little effort, I was able to swallow the full length of his swollen prick.

"Mmm, you're a good little cocksucker," he said through labored groans. "You like having my dick fed to you, don't you?"

I grunted my reply as he began driving his hips forward and fucking my throat. Looking up at him, I could see a vein protruding from his forehead and sweat forming at his hairline. He was really getting into it.

Ricky began fucking me faster, forcing his cock all the way inside, then pulling back, and pushing it forward until I'd swallowed him again. I loved the salty taste of his steady stream of pre-cum and judging by the way his legs were shaking, I figured he was close to rewarding me for a job well done.

Then abruptly, he stopped. "Okay, that's enough," he said.

A long rope of pre-cum formed a bridge between my swollen lips and his cock. I licked it away and asked, "Was I doing it wrong, sir?"

"No, Charles," he purred, rubbing the back of my neck. "You're doing a great job. In fact, you had me ready to blow my wad down your throat."

"So what's wrong with that?"

His brown eyes glimmered in the light. "Get up."

I stood, wincing at the soreness in my knees. The concrete had embedded its texture into my skin. Though I'd been ignoring it, my cock was still inflated and bulging with blood. "What now, sir?"

"Turn around and bend over the bed."

I swiveled my body and dropped forward to find support on my palms. Ricky ran his hand down the flesh of my butt. I broke out in a blanket of goosebumps. Now he was the one using the soft touch technique to torture me. It was so effective.

He traced a thumb down my spine, brushing against the thin wisp of blond hair that sprouts from the dark crevice of my butt cheeks. I spread my legs apart and watched over my shoulder as he leaned in for a closer look at my hole.

"That's a nice looking pucker you've got there," he said.

"Thank you, sir."

He probed me with his thick fingertips, tickling my hole. "Mmm, you feel nice and tight."

"I'm glad you like it, sir." This business of calling Ricky 'sir' was beginning to feel redundant and a bit silly, but every time I said it, I felt his approval wash over me. Submitting to him was addictive.

"Get on the bed now. On your knees and spread open so I can get in there."

I crawled onto the mattress and got into position. He leaned in and took a long sniff of my hole.

"You smell so damn delicious," he said.

"Thank you, sir."

He dipped his tongue between my cheeks and I trembled. With the second swipe, he went deeper, pressing against the tightness of my entrance. My muscles clenched, but he probed until they relaxed and the tip of his tongue began to wiggle inside.

My nuts were stuffed behind me, the head of my cock pressed into the bed like a stiff pole. His tongue glided down my taint, skated across my sensitive sack, and then along the underside of my cock.

"Oooh, yeah," I moaned into a pillow. I wanted more; wanted him to take my whole cock into his mouth so he could service me the way I'd serviced him. But all I got was a little tease with his tongue, then he returned back to my hole and devoured it.

My body relaxed and surrendered to him. Through breathless moans, I could feel myself getting loose and pliable as he worked his tongue inside. He began fucking me with firm, quick flicks of his tongue, in and out.

Nobody had ever eaten my ass with such hunger before. The sweet sensations seemed to ripple all through my body.

Ricky stopped and took a breath, smacked his wet lips together. "You ready for this dick, Charles?"

"Yes, sir. Give it all to me."

He grazed my spit-drenched hole with his pre-cum soaked cock head. I tightened instinctively, but he held the pressure until my muscles relaxed and the head began to sink in.

The union of my wet insides melding together with his warm, stiff cock was incredible. Getting past the tense outer rings of muscle took some effort, but once he broke past the barrier of my hole, his entire shaft was enveloped in my body.

A sharp tinge shot through my sensitive interior. His cock felt like a small fist being driven through me. But he forged on and with each thrust, the pain subsided and I welcomed him deeper inside.

Between heavy breaths, he groaned. "Ahh, you feel so good, Charles."

Our bodies worked in unison. My gyrating bottom pushed back against his hips as he thrust himself in and out with long, measured strokes. I tried to quicken the pace, tried to impale myself on his cock so I could control the timing, but he wasn't having it.

"Slow down," he said.

"But it feels sooo good."

He slapped my left ass cheek hard. "Don't forget who's in charge here."

"Yes, sir," I yelped, and stayed perfectly still so he had full control of my body.

Ricky continued his slow and methodical strokes, probing all the way inside until my hungry hole swallowed him down to his balls. Then he pulled all the way out until I was pried open with his flared tip. He just let it hang there as the lips of my hole hugged his cock head.

And repeat.

The rhythm was so maddeningly slow. The pressure had to be boiling in his balls, begging for release. But whenever his breaths became jagged and I sensed his cum was pummeling to the surface, he stopped until it settled.

I let out a frustrated whimper. My bound cock was leaking so much pre-cum that I'd formed a puddle on the sheets. Ricky grabbed a palmful of my slippery fluid, reached around to my face and smeared it across my mouth.

"You're a sticky fucking mess," he said gruffly.

"I know, sir."

"Lick my fingers clean."

"Yes, sir." I obediently lapped my sap from his fingers. It gave me a twisted sort of pleasure to taste myself on his skin.

"Alright, now flip over on to your back," Ricky ordered.

I rolled over and spread my legs open into the shape of a V.

He grabbed hold of my hips and railed back inside my stretched hole. His thick cock had a slight curve to it that pounded across my prostate gland with each thrust in and out of me. The angle was already driving me crazy.

I gripped the edge of the mattress so tightly, my knuckles were probably turning white. My entire body was humming with excitement, pleasure sensors activated in every cell.

Ricky must have liked the angle too because his soft moans became loud, primal growls. As he worked himself toward orgasm, he was bringing me closer to the brink with him. We were on this journey together.

He began riding me like a bull, fucking me hard and fast.

"Ah, yeah, here it comes!" Ricky called out.

His cock stiffened and swelled even larger and harder as he shot a hot load of cum deep inside my wet hole. He clenched his teeth, sweat dripping from his forehead, nostrils flared while he pumped me full.

The pleasure coursed through my body and it felt like I was elevated to a new level of ecstasy. I'd never had this much satisfaction before.

I began wailing as Ricky continued to pound away at my cum-filled insides. Then I felt a familiar quaking building from my balls. They were bound so tightly that they looked like two purple plums about to explode from the skin of my sack.

"Please, Ricky, I need to touch myself. I need to come."

He sneered deviously. "If you want to come, then do it."

I reached for my cock but he batted it away. "What was that for?" I asked.

"If you want to come, you have to let me fuck it out of you." He punctuated by slamming his rigid cock head directly against my sensitive, aching prostate.

I gasped as he did it again and again until I was delirious with pleasure and pain. I needed relief so badly.

Then I started to feel something different. It was the building crescendo to an orgasm, but instead of rising up to the head of my cock as it usually did, it seemed to be blooming from somewhere deeper in my core.

"Oh, fuck, Ricky... That feels so good."

"That's it. Just relax and let me take control." His voice was smooth but determined.

The orgasm soared inside me, climbing from level to level as my whole body shook. A nest of heat spread out from my prostate and blanketed my thighs, my nuts, and all the way up my cock until a blast of burning white cum exploded from me like a rocket. My release landed on my abs and my chest in thick globs. One shot hit me in the chin.

After we'd both been milked dry, Ricky collapsed beside me. The air was heavy with the smell of sex and sweat. Our spent bodies breathed in rhythm.

Without thinking, I rolled over and cuddled into his arms. "That was amazing, sir."

His body tightened, and I thought he was going to scold me for the spontaneous act of intimacy. But instead, he relaxed

again and pulled me against his heaving chest. "It sure was," he
agreed.

I reached down between my legs and began to unknot the
rope, which was soaked in fluids.

"What are you doing?" he asked.

"Oh, I thought it was okay to take this off. My nuts are
kind of aching... Sir."

Ricky looked at me as if he were contemplating whether
he'd let this power game go on long enough. Then he smiled
gently, caressed my face, and said, "At ease."

I freed my goods and fell asleep listening to the beating of
Ricky's heart against my ear, my thoughts hazy in the euphoric
afterglow.

Sometime during the night, he must have gotten up and
left without saying good-bye. I woke up at around two in the
morning, lying in the bed alone. A sadness grew inside me,
wishing we could have made plans to meet again. I wasn't
ready for our time to be over yet.

CHAPTER 3

The week ahead proceeded slowly. I found myself counting the days, hours, minutes, seconds, breaths...until it was Friday night again.

Finally.

I admired myself in the mirror, fresh shaven and clean. *Not bad.* I patted my cheeks and neck with the delicious scent of Aqua Velva, breathing in the cool menthol.

And then I wondered to myself: *will he be there?*

I shook away the thought. I'd been thinking about Ricky constantly since our encounter.

Little things. *Stupid things.* I'd be preparing a meal in the small kitchen of the guesthouse, boiling a crab fresh from my catch of the day. Then the image of the soldier would dart through my thoughts. I'd imagine planning a romantic candlelit dinner for two.

Again, *stupid things.*

It wasn't normal for a man to be daydreaming about cooking meals for another man, flitting about in the kitchen like a doting wife. It wasn't that I wanted to play 'house' with him. I just liked taking care of people. Food was one of the ways I showed I cared.

But it had just been sex with him. It had to be. There was no future for two men outside of the bathhouse. So I finished getting dressed in a fresh-pressed pair of khaki trousers and a white and navy blue striped sweater. It was another foggy and cool San Francisco summer night.

My blond mop was slicked back with hair grease. A new style I'd decided to try. Maybe Ricky would think it made me look cool.

There I went again, building up fantasies when I didn't even know if he'd be there, much less care what my hair looked like.

I headed over to the bathhouse. It was quiet. Still kind of early in the evening. I scanned the room casually when I walked in, nodded at a few familiar faces, then strolled to the locker room and changed out of my clothes.

Where was he?

I couldn't deny my only intention that night was finding Ricky. Nobody else mattered. My next step would have been to hit the showers and put on my little show. That was always my routine, even though I'd already showered at the house. On that night, I decided there was no need to put on a performance. There was only one man I wanted to impress. So instead, I took off my clothes and wrapped a fresh white towel around my waist, then went searching.

He wasn't in the sauna or the lounge area. I made a few laps around the building, trying to be casual.

Back through the locker room. Back through the showers.

My heart sunk as I began to realize he probably wasn't there. I didn't know why I'd been expecting him. It was just that I thought... Maybe...

It didn't matter.

My mood was soured and I didn't feel like messing around with anyone else. That was something very out of the ordinary for me. I figured I'd go back to my locker and get dressed, then head home. Or maybe go for a walk along the beach. Clear my head.

As I turned the corner of the main hallway, I bumped shoulders with Lenny. He smiled jovially at me, gave my butt a quick pinch. "Charles, good to see you!"

I smiled half-heartedly. "Good to see you too."

He slapped my bare chest with the backside of his fingers. "Why so glum, chum?"

"Oh, nothing," I said with a shrug. "Must be coming down with a bug."

"That's too bad. I was hoping we could do something tonight."

"You and me?" In all the times Lenny had flirted with me, he'd never suggested getting together. I wondered what the catch was.

"You, me, and a third," Lenny explained. "I've got that hot slab of military meat waiting in room twelve. Maybe we could make a sandwich out of him."

"You mean Ricky? He was ready to kill you last night."

"I know," Lenny said, biting his knuckles with excitement. "But I was able to sweet-talk him into giving me a second chance."

"Does he know you're asking me?"

Lenny shook his head. "No, but we can surprise him. Wouldn't that be fun? We can just come back to the room together and start licking him all over. I'll take the front and you can take the back. Or vice versa. Whatever you're into."

My catalog of moods was quickly flipping through the pages. At first, I was surprised, then confused, but now, something deeper and darker was taking hold. I felt warm in my cheeks and my stomach began twisting in knots.

It wasn't embarrassment. It wasn't nerves. It was something else.

I nodded. "Alright, lead the way."

Lenny took off down the hall and I followed behind him. I didn't want him to spend too much time looking at my face. I feared it would betray me and give him a hint of what I was really feeling.

Which was...

I still couldn't pinpoint the feeling. It was like angry sadness.

Why would Ricky waste his time on a clown like Lenny? Why would he spend time with anyone else but me?

Lenny opened the door and motioned for me to go ahead into the room. I faked my best smile.

Ricky was sitting on the bed when he saw me. His eyes widened with recognition. He looked happy to see me and that sent a flutter through my chest, mixed with my tangled bramble of foreign feelings.

I took in the sight of Ricky's sculpted body. He was nude except for the same white cotton uniform Lenny and I were wearing.

Lenny shed his towel first, hanging it on a hook by the door. "Look who I found," he said, beaming. "You two remember each other."

Ricky stood to greet me. "Of course."

I ignored him, turning to Lenny instead. "So you want us both, huh?"

"Uh, yeah," Lenny said, as if it were a dumb thing to ask.

"Let me get you warmed up." I grabbed a bottle of baby oil from the small bedside table and poured a generous pool in the palm of my hand, then took hold of Lenny's cock. He was hard in an instant and shuddered as I began vigorously stroking his lengthening shaft. "You like that, don't you?" I whispered.

Ricky began planting soft kisses on my shoulder from behind. I ignored his advances, focusing on Lenny as I worked his cock.

"Whoa, whoa, slow down there, partner," Lenny said between gasps.

But I kept going, squeezing and pumping his slick dick until his whole body began to stiffen.

"Cha-Charlie, wait, wait, too fast." But he showed no signs of pulling away so I kept stroking.

My plan was to wear him out early and then send him on his way so I'd have the soldier all to myself.

"Ah, fuck, I'm gonna shoot," Lenny groaned. A thick rope of cum burst from his cock and landed between our feet. I kept pumping, determined to make sure he would leave the room feeling completely spent.

Finally, Lenny wilted in my hand like a dandelion plucked from its stem. He pulled away. "Too sensitive."

The whole event must have taken less than two minutes. He stood there awkwardly with his floppy soft dick coated in oil and semen. He looked tired, confused, and a little angry about blowing his load.

"Why'd you do that?" Lenny asked.

That's when the answer hit me.

Jealousy.

The intense storm inside me, the sensation of anger and sadness duking it out, that was jealousy. It was an unfamiliar emotion, but so razor sharp that it consumed me.

I patted his bare belly. "Sorry, Lenny boy. I just couldn't hold back. I wanted your dick so bad."

A smile spread across Lenny's lips and his cheeks turned rosy pink with pride. "Ah, that's okay. I just wish you'd waited. I really wanted the three of us to play together."

"Maybe next time," I said, taking his towel from the hook and offering it to him.

"Yeah, okay." He nodded and cleaned himself off. "Well, you guys have fun. I'm going to take a shower and maybe go out. The cinema is playing a triple-feature of Rock Hudson films."

"The guy who's always playing a cowboy?" I asked.

Lenny nodded. "Yeah, but he's doing more serious stuff now. Romantic pictures. He's a real dreamboat."

"Okay, well enjoy." I scooted Lenny out of the room and then finally worked up the nerve to look behind me at Ricky. He had his arms crossed and a smirk on his face.

When the door shut behind us, I felt the anger simmering to a slow burn. We were finally alone, the way I'd pictured us all week. The fact that he'd been willing to have sex with someone other than me left a blemish on the perfect picture in my mind.

"You're quite a pistol, aren't you?" Ricky remarked.

"Well, I do feel like a loaded gun." I reached between the overlap in his towel and grabbed hold of his cock and balls, forming my fingers into a tight ring. "Did I say you could share yourself with other people?"

Ricky chuckled. "I didn't know we were going steady."

I tightened my grip. "Oh, you think you're funny?"

"No, but you are with this little act you're putting on." He seized my wrist and nudged me away from his jewels.

Something about his steadfast confidence bothered me. He seemed so certain he had the upper hand. And I couldn't blame him. After all, I'd been the submissive one who got on my knees and allowed him to have his way with me.

But I liked to turn the tables and surprise men. The bathhouse was an exhilarating opportunity for me to explore new identities; a stark contrast to the monotonous routines of my daily life. So I decided to go all the way to the other extreme and take on the role of the alpha dog.

I tightened my jaw and narrowed my eyes. "That's enough out of you, maggot!" I barked. "Tonight I'm the drill sergeant."

The smirk disappeared from Ricky's face. His back stiffened and he turned his gaze forward, standing tall and straight.

"That's more like it," I said. "Now take off your towel and report for duty. I'm going to give you a full body inspection and you'd better be squeaky clean, soldier."

"Yes, sir." He hung his towel and then stood in front of me with his arms down at his sides. The hint of a smile still lingered on his face, a sign that he was onto my game and willing to play along. I appreciated his versatility.

Earlier in the week, I'd stopped at the library to do some research. I learned that the Army had strict guidelines about hygiene. Soldiers were expected to report to duty clean-shaven, freshly showered, with teeth brushed and hair buzzed short. It

was considered disrespectful if they showed up looking
unkempt or smelling unclean. As a neat-freak myself, that
mindset perfectly aligned with my own credo.

Every muscle in Ricky's body was flexed as he stood there
waiting patiently. I examined his perfect face while he stared
unflinchingly at the wall. His jawline was square and hard as if
cut from steel.

I lifted his arm above his head, revealing the tight black
curls that grew in the scoop. I'd always been curious about a
man's armpits but never felt emboldened enough to explore
them. This felt right, so I decided to go for it.

Leaning into the slope beneath his arm, I deeply inhaled
his fragrance. He was fresh, as I'd expected, but there was
something indescribable about the humid environment. A
natural aroma that I wanted to drink in like a fine wine.

He shifted a little when my lips found his flesh. A minor
twitch, but otherwise he stood stoically. I dragged my tongue
from the muscular canvas at the peak of his ribcage up to the
heart of his armpit where I swirled around and took my time
tasting him. Then I moved north to the fleshy underside of his
bicep.

Ricky fought back a giggle that leaked out as a snort.

I reached over and twisted his nipple. "Is something funny,
soldier?" The nub grew hard between my fingertips and he
quivered again.

He suppressed a gasp. "No, sir."

I mashed his nipple between my fingers as if it were a balloon I was trying to pop. "Then why did you laugh?"

His knees seemed to buckle. "I'm just really sensitive under my arms and around my chest... Sir."

I released his reddened nipple and slithered around his body, brushing against his rigid erection. Pre-cum was leaking from the tip of his tight foreskin. It smeared against my leg, leaving behind a sticky snail trail. I ignored it and took my place behind him.

"Bend over," I commanded.

He folded his body forward. I crouched down behind him. With excited fingers, I spread apart his globes and took a long look at his hole. The tight knot puckered under my gaze, a telling sign that my steady and strong soldier was feeling a bit vulnerable and shy about such an intimate inspection.

I was feeling a bit vulnerable myself. My sexual encounters were usually so casual and disconnected. Perhaps we bathhouse men made a habit of remaining as aloof as possible. Digits inserted into holes; in, out, in, out, until the anticipated fluids were extracted and the participants were spent. Then a hearty slap on the shoulder like a baseball player saying, 'Good game, sport.' And it was all over.

But I was way past the point of being casual with Ricky. There was no denying it after my jealous display. So I went with the feeling and leaned in to greet his inviting hole.

Just a timid flick with the pointed tip of my tongue, testing the atmosphere like a snake. I licked him from the tender, fleshy underside behind his balls all the way up to the spread.

Ricky gasped softly. His composure was melting.

I licked his hole again, this time flattening my tongue into a pad, spreading it slowly up the same path. He moaned and let his stiff spine relax.

I probed deeper. We settled into a rhythm. I'd lick him, taste him, inhale the natural wonders of his flesh. He'd moan his appreciation, getting louder with more primal grunts that bellowed from the depths of his chest.

Soon his muscles began to loosen, opening the gates of heaven for me. I stiffened my tongue again and probed inside his delicious hole. Then I darted it in and out, fucking him with frenzied motions.

After soaking his hole in my saliva, getting it nice and wet and pliable, I acknowledged it with a wandering finger. Just the middle one, gently massaging Ricky's tight entrance, as if to say, *'Hello there, mind if I pop in for a visit?'*

He opened up for me without resistance. I slid inside slowly. My index finger, not wanting to be left out of the fun, chased after it.

Ricky's breath quickened as I found my way to his pleasure epicenter, rubbing gently in a circular motion around the swollen bubble of his prostate. Around, but not directly on it. I wanted to tease those oh-so-sensitive nerves that formed a web around the gland, giving him a little preview of what was coming.

I drove him around the block a few times and he began squirming impatiently. I knew he wanted my dick, but he'd have to wait.

"You like the way it feels when I play with your hole?" I was trying on some dirty talk to see how it fit.

"Oh, yeah," he groaned.

I thumped the core of his prostate. "Do you want me to fuck you with a bit more pressure?"

His breath seemed to catch in his throat as he murmured some semblance of a response.

"I can't hear you."

"Yesss," he groaned. Louder and clearer, he said, "Yes, fuck me hard. I want you, sir."

"Alright then."

I stiffened my pointers and worked in a third, my ring finger, to keep the other two company. Ricky was warm and wet and his body was stuffed full of me. I applied pressure directly to his prostate, pressing firmly at the top and then swiping all three fingers downward. Then I repeated the motion. With each swipe, his entire body shook.

"Okay, now go lie flat on your stomach and put your cock between your legs so I can see it," I instructed.

Ricky followed my lead and flattened down on the bed, pushing his big bull balls and bloated cock behind him. The glossy pink tip of his glans peeked out from his foreskin. He was so hard that he seemed to struggle to force his shaft down against the mattress.

Long ropes of crystal pre-cum were leaking from his wide slit. I wanted to make it flow faster, so I reached my fingers inside and pushed harder on his fun button. Another long rope of pre-cum pulsed out of him.

"I don't know how much more I can take before I come," Ricky said. "When are you going to fuck me?"

"I am fucking you, Ricky. Can't you feel that?" I twirled my fingers inside him and then pressed down in the center. He reacted with a loud, frustrated moan.

"Yes, and it feels great, but what about your cock? I want your cock inside me!"

I smiled devilishly. "Oh, well, I can't stick my big cock in you without some kind of lubrication, Ricky."

He looked over his shoulder and asked, "What about the baby oil that you used on Lenny?"

"Nah. If you want me to fuck you, you're going to have to make your own lubricant."

"What do you mean?"

Ricky didn't understand, but soon he would. I began working his hole with a feverish pace. His moans grew louder until he was practically screaming. I could see his cock twitching in response to my wicked persistence.

"Charles... Oh, fuck, Charles... Right there... Right there... It feels so..." A breathy sigh. "Sooo fucking good..."

His whole body tensed and tightened, then I felt his prostate gland harden against my fingers. Three quick shots of cum exploded from the shiny head of his cock onto the bed. I continued to stroke his tortured prostate until I'd forced out a couple more thick wads of milky white.

"Now I'm *really* going to fuck you, Ricky." I scooped up a hearty palm-full of his cum and slathered the hot, bubbly fluid all over my cock. "Turn over."

Ricky flipped onto his back with a look of dreamy afterglow on his face. "I don't know if I can take it," he said. "I'm really sensitive after I come."

"So you don't want me to fuck you now?" I asked.

A gluttonous smile spread across his mug. "Oh, I do, sir. I want all of you."

"Good." I settled onto the bed and spread his legs for easier access. "Just take a deep breath. I'm going to fuck you with your own cum."

We breathed together as I pressed myself into his spent hole. The air was thick with the bleachy fragrance of his homemade lube and the spicy sweat of our bodies.

I glided past his tight entrance with my cum-coated cock. The sensation of his sticky wet release combining with the soft, moist inner walls of his body felt so incredible, it was like slipping into a dream.

"You feel so good, Ricky," I moaned. "I'm going to fuck you full of my cum. Then our cum will be merged together inside you."

"Oh, yes," he said, craning his neck forward so his face was close to mine.

At first, I didn't recognize the gesture. It was so foreign to me. But as his lips found their way to mine, it suddenly seemed like the most natural thing in the world.

Timid at first, our mouths merged into a kiss. Then I sunk deeper inside as I pushed forward with my hips, and our bodies connected as one force.

Our tongues twirled and teased, then I burrowed further into his mouth, enjoying the sweetness of his breath. I couldn't get enough of him. Tasting him, feeling him, thrusting myself inside of his soft vortex. None of it felt like enough. I wanted to somehow merge my soul with his so we could share this intensity together.

Once again, I experienced a warm, fluttery feeling in my chest. *Was this love?* I wondered; that unfamiliar emotion I'd tried to hold at bay. I didn't know Ricky, so how could I love him?

But I wanted to know him. Everything about him. I wondered if the heart simply wants what it wants, with no burden of logic. After all, it's not the heart's job to be logical.

An electric current flowed between us, with our bodies mashed together, my hips jutting as I pummeled him. My heavy balls were stirring, an orgasm rumbling. It was heightened by the sudden onset of emotions I felt, ones I couldn't make sense of.

My breath quickened between our labored kisses. Ricky grabbed hold of my ass, digging his fingers into my flesh. His eyes were clenched shut.

"Look at me," I whispered.

His lids lifted and he stared into me. That vast golden brown terrain that filled his irises was almost too much, but I maintained eye contact, searching beyond the surface for somewhere deeper.

There was nothing to fear. I pulled him tighter against me, wrapping my arms around the solid sheet of muscle and bone that supported his back.

Hot liquid cum began burning the crest, ready to erupt out of me. My cock stiffened as I blew the first load inside his wet hole. I continued to thrust, pushing out another thick load, merging our semen together. Then came a third and fourth burst of white gold before I finally felt drained.

As we settled into the groggy aftermath, I kissed Ricky's lips, then his cheek, and ever so affectionately kissed him on the forehead. He started to pull away, freeing our sweaty skin from its tight lock. But I clung to him, holding my arms around him in a tight embrace.

"Just a minute," I said. "We need to talk about something."

CHAPTER 4

Ricky's face was filled with reluctance. "What's on your mind?"

I was reluctant too. Talking before sex was easy. All roads led to the same destination. It was simple. Uncomplicated. Talking *after* sex opened a door to endless possibilities. I released him from my arms and tried to squeeze into the tight space beside him.

"Here, let me make some room for you." He shuffled around in the bed, distancing himself from me with an invisible wall as I settled onto my back.

"Come closer." I put my arm over his shoulder and pulled him against me. Just moments before, we'd been kissing and clinging to each other. Now he was acting like a fidgety kitten that didn't want to be held. "I want to talk about my jealous outburst earlier. You know, with Lenny."

"Oh, that." His whole body seemed to freeze into a block of ice. "We don't need to talk about that."

"But I want to. I know I acted like we were... You know, *together.*"

"But we're not together," he confirmed.

The bluntness of his words hit like a hammer to my heart. I tried to smile through the pain. Tried to reason with him. "Look, let's both cut the tough guy act."

"We're men. We're supposed to be tough," he said sharply. "When I'm on duty, I have to guard myself twenty-four-seven. Always choosing my words carefully, always keeping my body stiff, always keeping my eyes on the ground. I can't let any slip-up give away my secret."

"Ricky, I have to be on guard too. How do you think the guys down at the docks would treat me if they ever knew?"

"Then why are you acting like we're a couple?" He stood up from the bed. I watched as his magnificent body glided toward the door to collect his towel. He was covered in the sticky remnants of our passion, and a perverse part of me didn't want him to wipe it off. The white crust that clung to the curls of his pubic hair seemed sacred.

"I just thought..."

"You thought what?" With a firm hand on his towel, he erased our memories from his skin.

I looked down at my hands intertwined in my lap and sighed. "Please don't be sore at me. I just thought we could start seeing each other more often. We could meet here, you know, at the end of the day. It could be nice, the two of us. We're safe here."

Ricky turned to face me from across the room. His soulful eyes glimmered in the light. For a moment, I thought those beautiful lips of his were going to part and he was going to share something profound and meaningful. But instead, he said, "I report for duty in the morning. I'll be in Taiwan for the next six months."

My heart sank into my stomach. "Oh."

"Yeah, 'oh.' Charles, what did you really think was going to happen here?"

I shrugged. "I don't know, Ricky. I've always been pretty content with my life, or at least I thought I was. Same routine, day in, day out. No real friends, no companion. One night a week, I came here and got to be a different person. But now you're in my life and suddenly one night a week isn't enough. I want more."

Ricky scoffed. "I can't give you more. I'm sorry. Even if we didn't have time and distance working against us, we're both men. We're different colors, we come from different worlds. There are places in this country where people don't even think my kind and your kind should be in the same classroom. No, I can't think of any way that wouldn't end without one or both of us getting hurt." He finished wiping his skin clean of us. Wiped away everything we'd shared. Then he wrapped himself loosely in his towel and opened the door, stopped inside the frame, and regarded me with a heavy stare.

I wanted him to come back to bed and hug me one last time. Give me one last kiss good-bye, if this really was good-bye. But instead, he served me a humble nod.

That wasn't enough. I stood and went over to join him in the doorway. "Ricky, wait, there's something special between us." He flinched when I put my hand on his shoulder. "I see the longing in your eyes. And listen, things are getting better out there. I know it's not my place to say that, but it's what I believe, damn it. Segregation is ending. Safe places like bars and bathhouse are becoming more common. We might be from different worlds, but our worlds are moving in the same direction. Let's find out where this goes when you get back. I'm willing to wait six months if it means we'll be together."

He caressed my cheek. I instantly felt my heart break.

"You'll be waiting a lot longer than that," he said. "I'm not coming back here. It's gotten too complicated. Take care of yourself, Charles. Oh, and um, I like what you did with your hair. You look like James Dean."

With that, the soldier walked out of my life.

CHAPTER 5

One month later

It's funny how someone can come into your life and turn everything upside down. I hadn't been the same since my whirlwind affair with Ricky.

We didn't know each other at all. Where did he grow up? What kind of music did he enjoy? All of those little things two people get to know about each other. It didn't make sense for me to be so hung up on him.

Maybe it was just the possibility... The 'what-ifs' about it all. I liked the way I felt when we were together. That was the only thing I knew for sure.

I knew Ricky was right when he said there wasn't a world out there for us. But I kept catching myself thinking, *there's a world for us in the bathhouse*. At least we'd have somewhere safe we could go. That had to count for something.

It was a rowdy Friday night at The Pacific and I was sitting outside in the hot tub. A month had passed and I hadn't been with a man since my soldier left. I knew it was absurd to save myself like some celibate priest, but I wasn't ready yet. So I just went out on Friday nights, trying to keep up my usual routine. It felt good to be around familiar friends.

Lenny was soaking in the water beside me. We'd never spoken about the way I behaved on that fateful night. He seemed to figure out that something deeper was going on, and thankfully he was kind enough to let it go.

It was only a little after nine o' clock when I decided to call it a night and go home. As I grabbed my towel, Lenny reached out and grabbed my arm.

"Hey, pal, where are you running off to?"

I looked at him curiously as I dried my legs. "What do you mean?"

"The night is young."

"But I'm getting older by the minute," I quipped.

"Well then I'll go get you a walking cane and we can take a stroll around the main room."

"Don't worry about it. I'm just going to go home and settle in with a book."

The owner, Jimmy, hurried out and nodded at Lenny. Something fishy was happening.

"What's going on?" I asked.

Lenny hopped out of the hot tub and wrapped a towel around himself. "I really think we should take that stroll."

He slung his arm around my shoulder and led me toward the door. Jimmy held it open for us, but he avoided eye contact as he tried to suppress a mischievous grin.

"Guys, what's this about?" I asked.

"Follow me," Lenny said.

We walked down the main corridor to the lounge area. My heart leaped into my throat when I locked eyes with my handsome soldier.

Ricky.

I'd never seen him in uniform and the view was stunning. But as my gaze traveled from his smooth face down his body, I realized something wasn't the same. He was supporting himself on crutches.

His left pant leg was pinned up at the kneecap so it wouldn't drag. There was only one brown leather boot on the ground.

My mouth fell open and emotions surged through me as I rushed over to greet him. "Ricky, your leg—"

Tears began to well in his eyes but he forced his teeth into a smile. "Who weighs twenty-five pounds lighter and gets his shoes at half price?"

I was in such shock, I didn't comprehend that he was trying to make a joke. "What—I—"

All I could think to do was pull him into my arms. "Ricky, what happened?"

"I wish I had some brave story about how I fought off the enemy and narrowly escaped, losing my leg in battle," he explained. "But in truth, it was just a dumb accident. I'd only been in Taiwan two days. We were running a parachute drill. I jumped out of the plane and my equipment malfunctioned. I crashed into the slope of a mountain and shattered my leg."

I took his face in my hands and wiped away his tears. "That's terrible. I... Ricky, I can't even believe it. You could have died."

He nodded. "All in all, I consider myself lucky that it was just one leg I lost. I'm still getting used to the idea," he confessed. "But the whole time I was away, all I could think about was the way I'd hurt you. I kept having dreams about you when I was in the hospital. I knew when I got back, I had to find you and make things right."

Now I was the one crying. "Ricky, are you saying what I think you're saying?"

"Yes. Charles, I'm sorry for how cold I was to you. I didn't want to admit that I was falling for you too, so I thought if I could hurt you, maybe you'd forget about me."

"I couldn't forget about you. I've thought about you every day since you left. So is this it for you? I mean, are you going back?"

"Losing a limb gets you an honorable discharge."

"Oh. Right." I smiled lamely. "Well, what happens now?"

"That depends." He pressed his soft lips against mine and kissed me long and deep. When we finally parted for air, he said, "I'd like to spend some time getting to know you. Maybe we could even try to be together outside of here."

Nervous energy fluttered through me. I felt like I was home again. I'd missed his touch, his kiss, the twinkle in his eyes. "My place is kind of small," I said, trying to think of ways to get him into the guesthouse without attracting too much attention from my employers. "But it's private and tucked away by the beach."

"I'm getting an apartment," Ricky said. "You could come see me there."

"That sounds perfect." I hugged him tightly against me, inhaling his fresh, clean scent and feeling the rough graze of his starched uniform on my bare skin.

"Why don't you get dressed and then we'll go somewhere and have some coffee?" he suggested.

"I'd love to."

Still stunned and taking it all in, I had a long look at the wounded soldier standing before me. Until I'd met Ricky, I'd never imagined a future with someone else in it. But that's the thing about the future: it's yours to re-write any time you like.

Everybody wants to be loved. That's what I believe. I'd hidden from love for so long, my heart had gone numb. But Ricky had thawed the ice and warmed me up to the idea of finding my own slice of happiness.

After I was dried off and dressed, I met up with Ricky in the lobby and slowly walked beside him as he hobbled out of The Pacific. I could tell he was struggling a bit to maneuver on crutches, but his pride would never let him admit it.

"Hey, soldier," I said with a sidelong glance, "did you learn any new rope tricks while you were away?"

His heart-shaped lips formed into a smile. "I may have picked up a few."

"Well, when you're feeling up to it, maybe we can try some more role play... Sir."

He reached for my left butt cheek and gave it a firm squeeze. "I'd love that."

We walked out together into the foggy San Francisco summer night. That's when our happily ever after began.

HOLLYWOOD
HEARTTHROB

CHAPTER 1

Los Angeles - August, 1955

It was a muggy summer night when Hollywood's leading man first walked into my life. He was wearing sunglasses even though it was pitch black outside, under the palm trees by the pool of the bathhouse. And even in the darkness, I could tell he was wearing a wig by the cock-eyed way it hung from his head.

"Getta load of this clown," I said, slapping my pal Vinnie on the shoulder.

We both looked over, past the dozen or so guys lounging in the water, and watched as the mysterious man in a thick white robe surveyed his surroundings. The way he walked was stiff. It kinda looked like he had a banana stuck up his butt and he had to move very carefully to avoid smashing it.

"Hey Rex, you think he's in the pictures?" Vinnie wondered out loud.

I nodded. "Probably."

It wasn't the first time some secret Mary had stumbled into the bathhouse. They all thought they were undercover like secret agents on a mission. But the truth was they stuck out like a sore thumb. I didn't know why they made such a big show of wearing silly disguises. It only drew more attention.

But this man was different. There was a quiet intensity that seemed to swirl around him. A sort of magic. I wondered what secrets were locked up behind his clenched tight jawline that seemed to be carved from stone.

A short, round man was escorting the robed celebrity. That's what really drew attention. The escort—bodyguard?—had a bald crown and was dressed in a suit and tie. He was probably the same height as a middle school student.

The little man whispered to the stranger. There was a good foot of difference in height between them, so the stranger had to crouch down to listen. He whispered something back. They both nodded, then turned and walked back toward the main building, where the private rooms, lockers, and lounge area were.

Vinnie and I looked at each other with confusion.

"Well, that was strange," he remarked.

I just shook my head and laughed. "Hollywood-types. They're all the same."

About that time, our friend Howard came flouncing outside and made his way over to us. He was a queenie type, with one hand over his mouth like an excited schoolgirl and his other wrist dangling in the air like a purse.

"Did you boys see him?" Howard asked.

"How could we miss him?" I said dryly.

"But you know who he is, right? From the westerns?"

A lightbulb seemed to come on in Vinnie's head and his lips spread into a smile. "You can't be serious."

I guess I was the dim one because I still wasn't in on the joke. Who were they talking about?

"That's him," Howard confirmed.

Vinnie said, "But he's doing kissy-kissy flicks now, right? I read in *Variety* that he has a new one coming out about a widow who falls in love with her gardener."

"Sounds like a yawner," I interjected. Love stories really weren't my thing. I preferred a good old-fashioned murder mystery. "And I still don't know who you're talking about."

"Let me give you a hint," Howard said with a coy giggle. "His name rhymes with cock and he's on his way to becoming Hollywood's new leading man."

Suddenly it all clicked, and although I wasn't usually the type to get star-struck, I did get a little weak in the knees thinking about him. "Get outta town."

"It's true," Vinnie said. "I hear he's been to some of the other baths too."

"But his days of sneaking around in anonymity are almost over," Howard explained. "He's becoming too famous."

I couldn't help but roll my eyes at that. If the man wanted to be anonymous, he probably shouldn't show up with his handler dressed in a three-piece suit.

Vinnie nodded back toward the door to the building and whispered, "Speak of the devil."

We looked over to see the round little man sweeping past the crowd and heading straight toward us. My whole body tensed up, feeling like the jokester in school who was about to be busted by the principal.

The man stopped beside me and looked down through his tiny glasses that perched on the tip of his bulbous nose. "You've been chosen."

I looked at Vinnie and Howard, seeking confirmation that this strange scenario was really happening. "For what?"

"Please come with me." The man turned on his heel and marched back toward the building.

A stubborn streak in me wanted to buck and stay put at the edge of the pool. But the other half of me felt tingly inside wondering if it really had been *him* in that white robe. My curiosity won and I quickly grabbed my towel and clumsily dried off while I hurried in. Vinnie and Howard were hot on my tail.

I swung open the tinted glass door just in time to see the little man disappear around the corner, headed toward the row of private rooms. The hallway was draped in shadows with only small sconce lamps on the walls to highlight the room numbers. If memory served me correctly there were twenty private rooms, ten on each side of the hall, and then five deluxe suites with extra amenities. It came as no surprise when we found ourselves at the sought-after corner suite.

The little man stopped outside the door and held his hand up. "Just you. The others need to go away."

I turned to Vinnie and Howard and shrugged.

"It's okay. We'll catch you later," Vinnie said, patting me on the back.

Howard smiled giddily and the two of them walked off, peeking over their shoulders several times.

The man turned the knob and pushed the door open. The main lights were turned out, but a small lamp glowed by the wet bar, which was stocked with bottles of wine, champagne, and soda.

"My name's Rex," I said, partly to the little man and partly to the dark silhouette sitting on the edge of the bed with his back to me.

The little man shook his head as he nudged me into the room and closed the door behind him. "Your name doesn't matter, sir."

That stung a little. I was just being polite. But in places like this, it was true. Names didn't really matter.

So there we were...alone. Just the two of us. I stood awkwardly inside the room, dressed in only a black pair of swim shorts with a dripping white towel hanging on my arm. I wasn't sure what to do next.

"Take off your clothes," the mysterious stranger commanded.

CHAPTER 2

I did as I was told, sliding the wet shorts off my body, and set them on a hanging rack to dry. Next to the bar was a door left ajar with a light shining from inside. A private bathroom, I assumed. The suite had everything. I was impressed.

Uncertain of what to do next as I stood there naked, wet, and cold, I walked over toward the bed.

"I'm a big fan of your pictures, Mister—"

"You have me confused with someone else," he said gruffly.

Because I'm a slow learner, I plowed ahead. "No, I'm very good with faces. I'd recognize you anywhere."

That was a fib. I hadn't recognized him until Howard pointed out his identity. But seeing him up close and personal, I had no doubt who I was standing next to.

He turned to me with his chiseled jaw clenched tight. A menacing look in his dark eyes. "Let's skip the small talk, pal. I said you have me confused with someone else."

"Oh, right." I was finally catching his drift. "My mistake. Sorry about that."

His shoulders seemed to relax a little as he sighed. He'd gotten rid of the silly wig and his perfect pitch-black hair was parted on the right side and neatly combed into waves. He must have fixed it after he got to the room. I reached out to touch him, but he flinched, grabbing hold of my wrist. "Have a seat on the bed."

I settled on the edge next to him. The mattress was softer than anything I'd ever sat on, like a cloud. My body sunk down into the cushy padding.

He rose up and stood in front of me, opening his white robe to reveal his naked body. His chest was canvassed in dark hair. He had a nice build, clearly someone who took care of himself, and a thick cock that hung over two balls the size of eggs. I admired a man with meaty balls.

I leaned forward into his body, taking in the spicy masculine scent of aftershave that wafted down from his clean-shaven face. Starting with his nipples, I licked and twirled my tongue on the right one until it perked up to a hard nub. He stood stoically in front of me as if he were trying very hard to suppress a reaction.

That was fine. I didn't mind a challenge. I moved on to his left nipple, making love to it with my mouth, licking it, then teasing it with a little nibble. An involuntary twitch betrayed him.

He pushed down on my head, his not-so-subtle way of telling me to move south. Clearly not a man interested in foreplay, so I slid a hand under his sack and gently licked circles around his right nut, then his left.

There was no reaction, so I turned my attention to the glossy crown of his cock and tickled it with the tip of my tongue before fully engulfing it in my mouth. It swelled to life as I swallowed it into my throat, filling me like an expanding balloon.

Now we were getting somewhere. It satisfied me to finally get a little non-verbal affirmation.

I looked up at him as I serviced his cock, watching his Adam's apple rise and drop in his throat. His eyes were clamped shut. I wondered what he was imagining, but it didn't matter. I was throat-fucking Hollywood's hottest star and I felt halfway to the moon about it.

Wrapping my hand around the hairy base of his shaft, I really started to get into it. We were settling into a rhythm and he'd begun to rock his hips in unison each time he went in and out of my mouth. I tightened my lips around him like a vacuum, sucking hard as he pulled out to just the tip, then he pushed back into my mouth again, jamming his long, thick cock past my tonsils until my nose was buried in his bush.

Then he stopped abruptly. "That'll be enough."

"What?"

"Lie down on your stomach."

I pulled back the sheets on the bed and sunk deeper into the cloud that served as a mattress. My cock was as solid as a piece of granite, so I tucked it underneath me to keep it from getting smashed.

"No!" he barked at me. "I don't want to see that."

"My cock?"

"Put it out of view."

"Sheesh," I whispered under my breath, pulling my dick back up against my abs.

I watched over my shoulder as he shed his robe and draped it over a sitting chair. He was a tall drink of water, probably well over six feet from what I could guess, and had a long, lean muscular frame that took my breath away.

The bed sank as he settled his knees on either side of me. Then I felt his hard cock being pushed between my butt cheeks. He was wet with my saliva and his pre-cum.

The hard helmet head of his cock breached the ring of my tight hole. He didn't seem interested in taking it slow or using his fingers to open me up, and I didn't dare ask. I bit down on a pillow as he mercilessly thrust inside me, all of his length at once, and my insides burned with agony.

He grunted as he pulled out to the tip, giving my sore insides a brief rest, then pushed forward again. This time was smoother and I could feel his leaking pre-cum coat the walls of my hole. The weight and heat of his body mixed with his sexy smell and soon I found myself in a dizzying state as he proceeded to fuck me hard.

After the fifth or sixth thrust in and out of me, the pain had melted away and then all I felt was the wonderful fullness of his cock. He was breathing heavily in my ear, his mouth lingering over my neck as he took command. I wanted him to kiss my skin, to trace his tongue down my shoulder, but this was purely an animalistic fuck.

So I settled into the pillow as my own hard and leaking cock lay neglected beneath me. He began going at it harder, driving his cock all the way to the root. His sweaty low-hangers slapped against my thighs. He grazed against my prostate with each thrust, sending tingles through me.

"Oh, yeah, that feels so good," I moaned.

He put his big hand across my mouth to silence me. "Shut up."

I should have been offended, but his brutal assault only seemed to turn me on more. He didn't want to see my cock, didn't want to hear my voice, and didn't want to see the look on my face as he fucked me. I was beginning to get an idea of what he was trying to pretend when those dreamy chocolate brown eyes of his were clenched shut. But I didn't care. He could pretend I was his wife and fuck me raw every night if he wanted. I'd take it.

Still covering my mouth to silence my involuntary grunts, he used his other hand to steady himself on the bed as he began fucking me like a wild animal. I could tell he was close. His body was getting slick with sweat, pressed against my skin, and he was pumping faster and faster.

Then he tensed and tightened against me and his cock seemed to expand in my hole. He blasted a thick load of cum deep inside me, then shot another two or three rounds, filling me to the brim. When he'd finally pumped himself dry, he let go of my face and collapsed on top of me, allowing himself a moment of surrender as he panted breathlessly.

I was so turned on, all I wanted to do was roll over and get myself off. When he unpinned me and stood up from the bed, I thought that was what would happen, but instead, he grabbed a fresh towel and wiped himself down, cleaning off the sweat and fluids, then he grabbed his baby blue button-down shirt from a hanger in the small closet and put it on. Next came his white jockey shorts, and his black slacks.

I rolled over onto my back and watched him. "I had a good time."

He grunted something that sounded vaguely like an acknowledgment, but he wouldn't look at me.

Was he angry?

No, ashamed. That's what this was. He was embarrassed about fucking a man.

When he'd finished getting dressed, he forced that ridiculous wig back over his head, put on his sunglasses, and stomped out of the room without even giving me a second glance.

Then I was alone, left in a mess of tangled sheets that smelled like him. I dipped my fingers between my butt cheeks and scooped out a bit of the sticky cum that was seeping from my bruised hole. It was still warm. I sniffed it, enjoying the familiar bleach-like scent, and licked it from my fingers. It tasted tart and salty. The nectar of a Hollywood heartthrob.

CHAPTER 3

I wasn't sure how long I was allowed to stay in the suite, but I decided to take full advantage of the private shower. Once the haze began to clear, the idea of what had happened really began to sink in.

It was him. Really him.

He'd used me like a hole in the ground. Like I meant nothing at all. And I didn't even mind.

The shower was a stand-up stall with white tiled walls and a glass enclosure. It was already steamy and wet when I stepped inside. He'd taken a shower before our encounter.

When I was sucking his cock, I could smell the fresh fragrance of soap on his skin. I appreciated a clean man. It meant he took pride in his hygiene. But truth be told, I would have sucked his cock even if it were caked in day-old sweat and dried piss.

Reaching for the bar of soap that sat on the ledge, I noticed it had a black hair embedded in it. The single curl must have washed off his body while he was lathering up. I collected the hair, examining it.

Should I keep it?

No.

I dismissed the idea as soon as it went through my head. What a crazy thing that would be to collect a celebrity's hair. But I was tempted.

Rubbing the bar all across my skin felt like a religious experience, knowing it was the same soap that had cleansed him. I started with my chest, rubbing it liberally around my hard pecs. My nipples grew hard as the hot water rained across them.

Then I worked my way down my abdomen, twirled a soapy finger inside my belly button, and settled into the nest of hair above my stiff, neglected cock.

I lathered up the entire area, soaping over my swollen balls. They were so sensitive, I trembled. Then I wrapped my fist tight around the bubbly base on my shaft and stroked upward. As I pleasured myself, I closed my eyes and imagined his cock was still inside me.

Using my free hand, I tickled the sore ring of my hole and dug in with my slippery middle digit. As the pad of my fingertip made contact with my prostate, the fantasy started to feel more realistic. My finger was his cock, probing deep inside me.

It didn't take long to make it to the brink. My prostate gland hardened against the push of my finger while an orgasm boiled through the core of my body. I looked down to watch as the first thick, white rope of cum exploded from the slit of my cock and blasted onto the glass door of the shower.

Goosebumps covered my flesh. A shudder rolled through me while I shot several more powerful bursts of semen. Then I milked the last drops from my spent cock. The aftermath was splattered all over the pristine glass.

As I panted heavily, trying to catch my breath, I suddenly realized I wasn't alone.

An older man stood in the doorway watching nonchalantly.

I covered myself by reflex, embarrassed by my graphic performance for a stranger standing only a foot away from me. "What are you doing in here?" I asked.

"Sorry to disturb you, sir," he said. The cleaning cart next to him explained why he was there. "I thought the suite had been vacated."

I haphazardly rinsed the soap off my body, trying to get clean so I could get out of there as fast as possible. But all I could focus on was the large white splotch that was melting down the panel of glass. I formed my hands into a scoop and tried to use them to direct water onto the door.

The janitor shook his head. "Don't worry about that, sir. Happens all the time. I'll clean it up."

"Oh, uh, okay." I finished rinsing away the soap from my skin and turned off the water. He offered me a towel from the stack on his cart.

I thanked him and wiped myself down hastily, then darted past him into the room to collect my shorts.

"Have a nice evening," he said as I made my way out of the suite.

"Thanks, you too." My cheeks were flushing red. I knew that I hadn't done anything wrong but that inherent shame still nagged at me. I breezed into the locker room to find Vinnie and Howard waiting on a bench. Their eyes lit up when they spotted me.

"Have you guys been waiting here the whole time?" I asked.

"Well, we were waiting down the hall from your room at first," Vinnie explained, "but that stuffy little bodyguard, or whatever he was, summoned the manager to come over and threaten to ban us."

"Walter said he'd ban you?"

We all knew Walter and he knew us. He was a friendly guy, pretty even-tempered, and I couldn't imagine him kicking us out.

"Yeah," Howard said. "I think he was pressured to do it, but it seems there's a rule against loitering outside the rooms."

I pulled my clothes from my locker and began getting dressed. "Well, privacy is important."

"If that big shot wanted privacy, he should have checked into the Ritz-Carlton," Vinnie said.

"Where a dozen reporters would have been waiting in the lobby?" I said with a scoff.

"Okay, I see what you mean," Vinnie conceded. "So tell us everything."

I felt like butterflies were dancing in my stomach. It took me back to high school when I had an intense infatuation with a jock named Bruno. I wanted to tell Vinnie and Howard everything, but something stopped me.

What happened was personal. Deeply private. Sure, it was a bathhouse. Sordid tales and gossip about conquests were considered fair game. But I'd been trusted with a secret and I felt the need to guard it closely.

It was obvious that I'd done *something* with the actor. The way he'd paraded through there in that ridiculous disguise only drew more attention to his identity. And Vinnie and Howard saw me go to his room with their own eyes.

But that's all anybody knew for certain. Nobody knew the details. They could make assumptions, make up stories, but only two people actually knew what happened. That felt sacred somehow.

My gut was guiding me so I shook my head as I slid on my brown loafers. "Sorry, boys, I'm going to keep it to myself. And I'd appreciate it if you didn't tell anyone what you saw."

Howard gaped and guffawed. "Rex, surely you're joking."

"Nope. This is different. He's a rising star and if word got out about this, it would destroy his career. He doesn't deserve that."

I didn't know why I was being so thoughtful after he'd treated me like a piece of meat. But somehow, I understood.

His fear of having his secret blown was about him, not me. He had a lot to lose.

"Did he tell you not to tell anyone?" Vinnie asked. Now came the negotiation tactic. He thought he was going to rationalize the truth out of me.

"No, but I think it's implied. In fact, he said he wasn't the person I thought he was. He told me I was mistaken."

Howard snorted. "And you believed him?"

"Look, I've said all I care to say. I hope you two can respect me and keep this under your hats."

I smiled at both of them, patted Vinnie on the shoulder, and strolled out of the locker room feeling good about myself. It would have been so satisfying to tell them all the juicy details, but keeping it a secret made it feel even more special.

On my way home that night, I passed a magazine stand where my Hollywood leading man graced the cover. It was a close-up of his face. Dark eyes staring right into me. I bought a copy and took it home to admire.

Yes, like high school all over again. I had a big crush on a man that could never be mine.

CHAPTER 4

I usually only went to the bathhouse once a week. Maybe twice
if I was feeling particularly lonely—or horny. It was my version
of a social life. Other men met up with their buddies to go to
baseball games or play poker. The bathhouse was where I
found relief.

But this weekend was different. One night wasn't enough.
I'd spent my Friday with a star and I couldn't resist going back
the next evening in hopes he'd return.

I knew it was a long shot as I sat there in the hot tub
steaming my coconuts along with Howard and Vinnie. They
must have sensed what I was up to because they stayed by my
side most of the night. We talked, tried to make casual
conversation, all without mentioning the big pink elephant in
the room. They were trying to respect my privacy, though I
could sense Howard was struggling to hold back all the
questions that were bubbling over inside.

My thirtieth birthday was coming up later in the week. I
was kind of in denial about it, but Howard, being the big
mouth that he was, had to bring it up. I suppose that was my

penance for him not bringing up my celebrity encounter. The man couldn't be expected to keep all my secrets to himself.

Getting older didn't really bother me. I just felt kind of stuck. I'd been working the same monotonous job as a banker since I was twenty-two. The hours were steady, the pay was good, but I didn't have much of a life outside of work. The bathhouse was the most exciting part of my week.

Howard and Vinnie began insisting on throwing a party to celebrate my big day, but I wasn't having it. We debated for a little bit, then they finally let it go.

Our eyes were always on the back door of the patio. Every time the door opened, my heart jumped into my throat. At around eleven-thirty, we finally decided to call it a night. Our skin was wrinkled like prunes after spending the whole evening alternating in and out of the water. We hadn't even paid attention to the tasty prospects parading around the swimming pool.

We were back again on Sunday night. Silly, I know, but I felt better being there hoping he'd return rather than staying home and wondering if I'd miss out.

Of course he didn't show.

Howard couldn't join us on Monday night. Mondays were when he volunteered at a nursing home playing piano for the residents. I admired him for that. Vinnie was nice enough to come and sit with me, although he did excuse himself for a little while to spend some time in a private room with a handsome young fella he'd been eye-fucking for an hour.

By Tuesday, I was feeling pretty ridiculous, so I phoned both Howard and Vinnie to tell them there was no need to make a special trip out just for me. I stayed by the pool until about ten that night, then finally gave up.

It was on Wednesday night when my persistence finally paid off. I decided to spend the evening resting in a lounge chair since my poor skin was dry and itchy from all the time I'd spent in the water the past few evenings.

I was lying there under the full moon and stars, listening to the breeze rustle the palm trees above me. Only a few other guys were outside in the pool. It was getting late on a weeknight, so most men didn't stick around past nine.

The door squeaked open. I hardly noticed it and my neck was sore from constantly craning over to see.

But there he was.

Same stupid wig, same stumpy bodyguard walking beside him. With his eyes covered in thick sunglasses, I couldn't tell where my heartthrob was looking, but I sensed his gaze brushing over me. Then he leaned in and whispered something to his bodyguard and turned to walk away.

My heart was pounding as I sat up anxiously in my chair, expecting the little round man to come over and tell me I'd been chosen...again. But instead he made his way to a young blond boy, probably just out of high school, who was busy tossing a colorful beach ball back and forth with his friends.

The dumb kid hadn't even noticed the star and his bodyguard sweep through the joint. I could tell he was confused when the bodyguard knelt down at the edge of the water to tell the young man to come with him.

At first, I could see the apprehension, but the bodyguard kept talking, and he must have said the right thing because the kid finally got out of the pool and dried off.

I wondered if he'd been offered money. Would the most eligible bachelor in Hollywood pay for sex? That didn't seem to add up, but maybe it was more about paying for discretion.

The young man walked away with the handler and I watched helplessly from the sidelines. An intense wave of heat began flowing through me. At first I thought it was just the air, then I realized it was coming from inside me.

I was jealous.

Why hadn't I been chosen? Was I not good enough? Not young enough?

I was in pretty good shape for someone who was about to turn thirty. Okay, so I wasn't quite as lean, toned, and perky as the blondie who'd just been summoned. But I offered experience, and most of all, I had gratitude. That dumb kid didn't even notice the legend when he walked through the door.

Before I even realized what I was doing, I'd already jumped up from my chair and found myself barreling down the interior hallway toward the private suites. Logic and caution were far out of reach. I was operating on red-hot passion. After wasting night after night waiting outside by the pool, I wasn't going to lose my shot to some kid.

The bodyguard's eyes bugged out when he saw me coming toward him in the hall.

"I'm going in," I said through gritted teeth.

The bodyguard's calm, professional demeanor changed to that of a high-voiced queen with her hair on fire. "Noooo, you can't go in there!" he squealed.

"Out of my way." I nudged him aside and turned the doorknob. Surprisingly, it hadn't been locked. I figured maybe it was left accessible in case the bodyguard, if you could call him that, needed immediate access to rescue the actor.

The bodyguard scurried off, presumably to find the manager.

My dream man was sitting in a black leather armchair with wet hair and a white robe on. The bathroom door was closed and light spilled through the edges.

The actor stood up, all six feet plus of him, and his shoulders stiffened as he plucked a cigarette from his mouth. "What's the meaning of this?"

In a flash, I was standing close enough to smell his soapy, clean skin. "I've waited all week for you and I'm not sharing," I said.

Instead of anger, he smirked. His sexy lips raised. "Is that so?" His voice was velvety, sounding more like the natural tone I'd heard in his movies rather than the tense, clipped syllables he spoke to me during our first encounter.

"Yeah, that's right," I said. My fists were clenched, though I didn't know why. Maybe I was preparing to spar with that young blond dope. "Why don't you send the boy away and let me show you what a real man can offer."

The bathroom door flew open and the young man stood there with a towel around his waist, looking at me with astonishment. On cue, the flailing excuse for a bodyguard came running back in with Walter, the manager.

"What's going on in here?" Walter asked.

"Nothing, just a little misunderstanding," the actor said coolly.

I was afraid he was going to have me kicked out of the bathhouse, probably banned permanently, but instead he looked over at the blond and said, "This fella was just leaving."

The young man looked indignant. He grabbed his wet swim shorts from the bathroom and stormed out.

"Sir, wait," the bodyguard said, running after him. If he had been paying for the young man's silence, he was probably about to double, even triple the offer to smooth things over.

"You're sure everything's okay in here?" Walter asked.

The actor smiled assuringly. "Never better. Thank you for checking on me."

"Okay," Walter said, eyeing me as he walked out, and closed the door behind him.

Alone at last.

The sexy actor studied me with amusement in his eyes. My bold move was paying off. In fact, I thought he might be impressed by my tenacity.

I stepped out of my swim shorts and settled onto my back in the bed made from clouds.

He took a long drag from his cigarette. Smoke rolled from his nostrils like a dragon as he took off his robe. "Turn over onto your stomach. You know how I like it."

I lifted my legs in the air, spread open wide. "No, I want to see your face when you blow your load in me."

He grunted and took the cigarette from his mouth, mashed it into an ashtray, then strolled over and got on the bed. I felt the springs sinking around me as he grabbed hold of my legs and hooked them over his shoulders.

I'd awakened something carnal in him.

He spat in his hand, rolled his wet palm across his cock, which was already hard and standing straight up at attention. Then he spat on my spread ass cheeks, not really bothering to aim for my hole. Just the general vicinity.

That was how he was going to punish me, by fucking me with hardly any lubrication. But I remembered he was quite a pre-cummer, so I was sure my hole would be nice and slick within a few thrusts.

I didn't care as long as I had him in me. He could fuck me dry and use my blood as lubricant if he wanted.

The first thrust hurt the worst. His large glans broke past the tight outer ring of my hole and shoved deep inside me with one movement. I clenched my teeth and kept my eyes locked on his. He was testing me.

When he pulled out, I could already feel the trail of pre-cum dripping from his cock, wetting me inside. He bucked his hips and plunged into me again, gliding in much more smoothly. But it still hurt. My tender insides burned and ached, but I did my best to hide it.

He settled into a rhythm, thrusting in and out as his cock leaked an endless supply of natural lubricant straight from the tap. The pain subsided and he had me positioned at just the right angle to ensure he was banging against my prostate.

I sat upright as best I could, given that my ankles were level with his face. I felt folded in half but the position was perfect to press my cock against my stomach. It provided a nice amount of friction when my sensitive cock head pressed against the soft patch of brown hair at my navel. Combined with the relentless pounding of my swollen insides, I was getting enough stimulation to coax an orgasm out of myself.

Our eyes remained locked as ripples of pleasure rolled through me from the front to the back, inside and out. His thick mop of jet black hair had fallen across his searing eyes. He was always so immaculately groomed on screen, but now I was getting to see him unkempt and free from all worries. Something about me must have put him at ease because he became louder and more expressive, grunting and groaning while he jackhammered his big cock in and out of me.

I could tell he was nearing an explosive climax by the way the skin of his collarbone flushed red and the vein that bulged from the side of his throat. Something was stirring inside me too. I'd never shot my load this way, not touching myself, just the rubbing sensation of my skin against skin. It was a new and almost foreign sensation, but the impending release was familiar as I felt it racing to the surface from behind my balls and rising toward my shaft.

Then we both screamed out as we shot our loads together. Burning hot cum burst from my cock as I felt the head of his cock swell and explode, filling me up. He wore a look of surprise on his face as my semen splashed against his hairy stomach. I could tell he didn't know I was about to come.

He pulled out of me and released my legs from his shoulders. His cock was still dripping with his creamy pearl-tinted release.

"Lick me clean," he demanded.

He pushed his wet crotch in my face, smelling of sweat and sex. I rolled my tongue along the head, sucking the remaining cum out of his slit like a straw. He shuddered, obviously feeling a little hypersensitive post-orgasm. I knew how sensitive my cock was after I came, so I could imagine how his felt.

But he persisted, pushing himself past my lips and filling my mouth. I licked up and down and around his shaft. Then I licked under the carriage and around his heavy balls before making my way up his treasure trail of dark hair to clean off the load I'd shot on him.

My cum was thick and gooey, already beginning to dry in the fibers. But I licked him thoroughly clean, all around his tight stomach, then I twirled the tip of my tongue around his belly button. He let out an involuntary giggle, showing me a softer side to the stone-cold façade. But he cleared his throat and the mask drew over his face again. All business. No fun.

"That's good enough." He pushed me off him, looking away, and got out of bed to collect his robe.

"Why don't we take a shower?" I offered. "We can give ourselves some time to recover and then go for a second round."

"I don't think so." His tone was harsh, his words were clipped again.

"Okay," I said softly, getting out of bed on the opposite side so we wouldn't cross paths. After I slid on my shorts and collected a towel, I headed for the door. "I guess I'll be going then."

His back was turned to me when he said, "Same time tomorrow night?"

I broke into a wide smile, though he refused to turn around to witness it. "Yeah, absolutely."

"Just come here to the room," he said.

"If I may offer some advice..."

"What is it?"

"You should come without that weird goon. He draws a lot of attention. And don't wear those wigs and sunglasses."

"How do I avoid being recognized?" His voice was gentler. He seemed to appreciate that I was taking his secret seriously.

"Wear a pair of thick black-rimmed eyeglasses. Those will alter your appearance quite a bit. It seems to work for

Superman, anyway. And maybe a fake mustache, but get a good, quality one from the studio."

He turned around and opened his mouth, presumably to once again claim he wasn't who he was and say he didn't work at a studio. But he seemed to think better of it, tightened his mouth, and just nodded.

"Have a nice evening," I said with a newly found optimism. And though I may have imagined it, I could swear I caught a glimpse of a smile forming at his lips.

"Night," he said plainly.

CHAPTER 5

Walking into the bathhouse the next evening felt like a completely different experience. Instead of being my usual social self, stopping to chat with friends along the way, I swept through the building like a ghost. *Is this how he feels all the time?* I wondered.

It was a lonely, empty feeling, as if all eyes were on me when I didn't want to be seen. I kept my head down and watched my loafers on the floor, turned right at the short hallway that led to the private suite, and didn't even bother making a stop at the locker room. There were too many familiar faces there, and I couldn't risk the questions if anyone had caught on.

The bodyguard wasn't outside the room. That was a relief not to have to deal with him again. I tapped on the door, lightly with the edge of my knuckle. There was a quick shuffle of bare feet on the other side, then the door opened just a hair.

I looked around me, confirming nobody was passing by, then whispered, "I'm alone."

The door opened a little farther but he'd stepped behind it. I slid inside and closed it, then turned the lock. He looked at the doorknob, then at me, and seemed to hesitate. He probably wasn't used to being alone and vulnerable.

"You're a sharp dresser," he said, eyeing my crisp white button-up shirt and navy tweed blazer.

"Thank you," I said, taking stock of his exposed body, clothed only in black wisps of hair and the white towel around his waist. The fabric was thick and luxurious; a premium grade of cotton much better than the thread-bare towels we were given in the locker room. "I think you're overdressed."

He smiled and pulled at the side of his towel. It melted at his feet. His skin was bronzed, much darker than it had been the night before. He must have spent the day in the sun. No tan lines either. He was already hard, his long cock standing tall to welcome me.

"That's more like it." I shed my jacket and plucked open the first button at my collar.

"Let me," he said, placing his hands at my neck and popping open the second button of my shirt. His face was only inches from mine as he made his way down my body. Disrobing me felt like such an intimate gesture, like we were lovers and he was greeting me after a long day at the office.

Who was this man? He was behaving like a completely different person. Someone gentle and kind. His eyes were on me, open and bright. I could see all the details too. The deep amber highlights that seemed to burst from the middle of each iris and the dark coffee-colored edges that framed them. I wasn't used to him looking at me that way. In fact I wasn't used to him looking at me much at all. He made my knees feel like jelly.

His warm hands connected with my skin as he tugged down my slacks and underwear.

"Have a seat on the bed," he said.

I stepped out of my shoes and followed him over to sit down. He knelt in front of me, took my right foot in his hands, and unrolled my sock.

"You have nice feet," he said.

"Oh, uh, thank you."

He began to massage the back of my heel, then worked his way down and spread his fingers between my toes. Then he did the same with my left foot and kissed the top surface.

I pressed my toes into his lap. "Do you like feet?"

"Sometimes."

This was foreign territory for me. I wasn't used to having my feet massaged, nor was I prepared for him to suddenly be so submissive. I asked, "How do you want me tonight?"

His gaze smoldered when he replied, "On top."

"You mean..." I raised an eyebrow and watched him crawl onto the bed to lie down next to me.

To clear up any confusion, he spread his legs apart, revealing the dense forest of dark curls between his ass cheeks.

Not missing a beat, I rolled over on top of him, pressing our hard cocks together. A tingle swam through me. I loved that feeling of the sensitive, fleshy underside of my cock rubbing against the sensitive, fleshy underside of my partner. It was one of my favorite ways to engage in foreplay.

I formed a fist and began pumping our cocks together. His skin was hot against mine. Then I leaned into him as he was raising his head up.

We kissed.

Our lips joined simultaneously without thought. It just felt natural in the moment.

I explored his mouth with my tongue. I'd expected him to taste like tobacco, but instead he tasted like toothpaste. I didn't care much for the taste of tobacco so I appreciated that he'd brushed his teeth.

Then I moved down to his neck, licking the tight muscle down the side.

He gasped softly. "Don't leave a mark, please."

"I won't."

His body relaxed as I moved downward to his chest, tracing swirls around each nipple with the tip of my tongue. He squirmed a little as I tickled him. I enjoyed the feeling of having power over him.

I kissed a path down to his crown of pubic hair, but instead of going for his swollen cock, I eschewed the obvious and buried my face behind his balls, taking the route to his bottom instead.

Spreading his cheeks apart, I found he had a tight pink hole that puckered shyly. I flicked my tongue across it, which made his cock jump. A steady stream of pre-cum was already flowing from the tip. I ignored it.

Instead, I delved deeper into his tight hole, tasting the clean, natural smell of his body. He moaned in response, a little louder than his normal, strangled tone that was locked down and guarded. I probed on, wetting and relaxing those tight sphincter muscles until I'd worked the tip of my tongue inside.

I loved the taste of him. I would eat his hole every day if he wanted. He seemed to be enjoying it too. When I peeked up at him, he'd rested his head against a pillow and made himself comfortable in the bed, so I continued licking and slurping at his wanting hole.

With his muscles relaxed, I slid my middle finger inside his tight, hot body. I found the firm bubble of his prostate gland and pressed it like a button. Another thick strand of fluid drooled out of his cock. It became a little game. I'd press, he'd moan and drip some more. I increased my pace, pushing firmer and faster until I was fucking him with the pad of my finger.

"I can't take it anymore," he breathed out. "I need you inside me."

I grinned triumphantly. *He*, this mega movie star, was begging *me* to fuck him. I loved it. "Alright then." I gently pulled my finger out and reached for some K-Y jelly that was on the table by the bed.

He must have planted it there. I didn't recall there being any lubricant beside the bed during our first two encounters. It sure could have helped when he was fucking me raw.

I could have been vindictive and ignored the tube of K-Y. I could have fucked him with only a bit of spit and grit as lubricant, the way he'd fucked me.

But no. I wanted to make him feel good. *Really good.* So I lathered up my cock, making it glossy and smooth with a generous glob of jelly. Then I carefully pressed my cock head against his wet hole, feeling the tender kiss of its lips against my glans.

"You ready?" I asked him.

He nodded vigorously.

Of course he was. I just wanted to draw out the anticipation a little longer.

I eased myself into him, nice and slow. A completely opposite approach from the way he'd stabbed himself right into my screaming hole the night before. Not that I minded, but the mood was different. A wall had come down. Maybe for the first time in his life, he was allowing himself to submit fully to another man.

My cock slid inside him, inch by inch. He was very tight, like a vice clamping down around me, but I eased my way in. He was watching me with pensive eyes.

"What are you thinking about?" I asked. Not exactly pillow talk, but I genuinely wanted to know.

"Just how good you feel inside me."

I smiled, savoring the soft, silky way his body fit me like a glove. "I like the way you feel too."

We reached the root of my shaft. My hard cock was buried like a bone and our bodies were connected as deep as I could go. That didn't stop me from thrusting my hips forward, trying to sink even deeper somehow. This magnetic energy was swarming between us and I wanted to feel as close as I could possibly get.

I leaned in and looked into his eyes. He seemed tentative, almost startled by the intimacy, but the creases softened at the edges of his eyelashes and suddenly it seemed like I was looking into his soul.

Our tongues danced, my upper lip taking gentle swipes against his mouth. The rough stubble of his face raked against my clean-shaven skin.

It appeared that he'd skipped shaving that day. He always presented himself as freshly groomed, but it seemed he wanted to be different with me. More real. I didn't mind.

His dark mop of hair was a bit of a mess too; still parted on the right side with a generous amount of Vitalis straining to hold it in place, but as he moved against the pillows, he began to take on a more tussled appearance.

I found myself wishing I could see that fresh-out-of-bed look on him every morning.

He took hold of my hands and laced his fingers between mine. I gave a firm squeeze while our kisses went deeper and our bodies rocked in harmony. Our breath was labored, our skin getting slick with sweat.

"I want us to come together," he murmured against my lips.

"Alright." I let go of one hand and reached between us to grip his hard, leaking cock. Using his own fluid as lubricant, I began working my palm up and down his shaft, giving an extra squeeze when I reached the sensitive flared head of his cock while I was pulsing in and out of him at the same time.

An orgasm was building in me, and I could tell by his moans that he was getting close too. So I shifted my angle just enough to ensure I was really hitting his prostate with each move. His moans became loud rumbles of pleasure against my lips.

With our mouths joined together, our limbs entangled, and our bodies connected, I pumped faster on his cock while pounding the orgasm out of him from the inside. All the friction against my sensitive cock brought me to the edge, and when I felt his body begin to quiver, I let go of my load and exploded inside of him just as he let go of his and shot a burning hot handful of cum into my hand.

I milked us both until there was nothing left inside. Then with weary, ragged breaths, sweat-drenched skin, and tired muscles, I collapsed on top of him in the bed.

"You're incredible," he whispered.

"And you're a dream come true," I said through heavy eyelids.

I nuzzled my chin between his neck and his shoulder, drifting off to sleep wrapped in the warmth of our bodies. The last thing I remembered was the sound of him snoring softly against my ear.

A couple of hours later, I woke to the sensation of him sliding out from under me in the bed. I'd been fast asleep, and I was only just beginning to register the beautiful sight of this man tip-toeing away.

"Don't worry about getting up," he whispered. "You can stay the night if you want."

I checked my wristwatch. "It's just after midnight."

"Yes."

I smiled. "That means it's my birthday. I'm starting my thirties with you."

"I'll be joining that club in November." He knelt down on the mattress and gave me a long, tender kiss. "Allow me to be the first to wish you a happy thirtieth birthday."

"Thank you. Now why don't you crawl back in here and we can settle in beneath the sheets?"

A look of sadness flickered in his eyes. He stood up and turned his back to me. There went that protective wall again. Though it was invisible, I could already sense its cold stone presence.

"I thought you'd finally let me in," I said.

"I did."

"Then why does it feel like I'm standing out in the rain?"

He let out a long sigh. "You know we can't be together."

"Then why are we?"

He turned to face me, back stiff, ready to argue. He didn't like to be challenged. That was one thing that was true about him both on-screen and off. "This was very special to me, Rex."

My heart broke a little when he said my name. It was the first time he'd used it. "But?"

"But you know it can't go on. I shouldn't have even let it get this far. I never go to bed with the same man twice. It complicates everything."

"Then why did you?"

A crease formed between his eyebrows and I realized he wasn't even sure. After stumbling for a moment, he amended by saying, "I guess I was inspired by your display of jealousy. You say what you want and you just go for it. No apologies. I want to be open and free like you. I want to be that type of man so badly. But that would mean giving up everything."

"I'm not asking to walk down the red carpet on your arm."

He shook his head and began throwing on his clothes, seemingly unconcerned with the crusty bodily fluids that had dried in his pubic hair. "I'm sorry, Rex. I have to go. Please understand."

"So this is good-bye?" I was stalling. I thought if I could just get him to stop and think about it, maybe he'd consider seeing me again. "What we had tonight was magic."

"I know, but if we keep this up, the story will fall into the wrong hands. Besides, I'm starting production on a new film in the morning. I'll be busy for the next few months."

"You have to rest sometime, right? I could come to your house at night. Help you get to sleep." Now I was acting desperate. It was worth it if I could win him over.

"What's your favorite flower?" he asked abruptly.

Nobody had ever asked me that. I hadn't really thought about it. "Orchids, I guess."

He nodded as if that explained everything. "Beautiful, but complicated." His sad brown eyes washed over me. I thought he was going to kiss me, and maybe he was, but it seemed he was afraid I'd grab hold and never let him go. Instead, he opened the door and ducked out. His stage-prop glasses and mustache were still sitting on the bedside table.

EPILOGUE

First thing in the morning, I received a special delivery at my apartment. A vase overflowing with lush white orchids. The biggest blooms I'd ever seen. The card attached read:

Happy birthday, R

The single letter could have been interpreted as my name or his. Clever. Cryptic. Probably ordered by his personal bodyguard. That dumpy little man who couldn't harm a fly.

But the bodyguard served a purpose. He helped keep that wall high around the kingdom of secrets.

No matter who'd ordered the orchids for me, I knew who the instructions came from. What more could I want?

Outside the hallowed chambers of the bathhouses, there wasn't a place in society for two men to be together. Not in 1955. And especially not with a celebrity like him, an asset worth millions to the studio.

All I knew was that after drinking from the fountain, I would always be thirsty for more of him. And I couldn't escape my desire.

The image of his handsome boy-next-door smile was all around me. Theaters, television, magazines, billboards. His fame catapulted to new heights shortly after our brief fling. He was everywhere and nowhere at the same time, for I never crossed paths with him again.

That autumn, news broke that he'd married a woman. It seemed he'd chosen to start out his thirties by doubling down on a lie. The announcement crushed me. I don't know why I was so stunned.

With a new bride at home, I figured there was no chance he'd be sneaking out to the bathhouses again. Besides, I could never get involved with a married man. It wouldn't be fair to his wife. I carried enough guilt on my shoulders for my attraction to men. I didn't need to weigh myself down with adultery too.

A year later, I bought my first house. A little one bedroom bungalow along Sunset Boulevard. To my surprise, I received another bouquet of white orchids on my birthday. Same card but from a different florist and in different handwriting:

Happy birthday, R

I couldn't believe he'd tracked me down. I couldn't believe he'd remembered me at all. That re-lit the flame in my heart all over again, hoping it was a sign of something bigger. But he didn't call. He didn't stop by. It was a romantic gesture and nothing more.

His marriage only lasted a few years before ending in a bitter divorce. Sometimes I thought of trying to reach out to him. I wondered if he would finally be open to the idea of a relationship. But I also kind of liked the mystique of having a secret admirer.

I moved on. I even managed to find love outside the bathhouse. According to rumors, he did too.

Over the years, I called a couple of different places home. No matter where I relocated in the Los Angeles area, the brilliant blooms found me. I often wondered why. What was it about me that made such a permanent impact on him? I chose to believe that I'd unlocked some special piece of his heart. Maybe that was his way of thanking me.

Every year, the flowers continued to arrive on my birthday. Each time, a different flower shop and different handwriting, which made me think the orders were being dictated over the telephone and written by a store employee.

Every year, for thirty years. I received my last bouquet in 1985, when I turned sixty. I knew that he would be turning sixty that November, so I decided it was time to finally break my silence. I'd written him a letter and planned to send it along with flowers on his birthday.

The 1980s were a precarious era for our community. For a while, we were running from a monster we didn't know how to defeat. Not even doctors had all the answers. Friends and lovers were losing the fight every day. I got lucky, I guess. Despite a few scares, I always managed to outrun it.

He was not so fortunate. On a sun-kissed October day, a month shy of his sixtieth birthday, he lost the good fight. And the world lost its legendary Hollywood heartthrob.

I never got the chance to send him my letter. To say all the things I wanted him to know. All I have now is the memory of our very fleeting time together. Then again, I guess that's all we really ever have. Little moments frozen in time. That's what makes up life.

The memories of our time together will live on in me.

DEEP RELEASE

CHAPTER 1

The summer heat was getting to me. I'd staved off the fever for as long as I could but my body had reached its boiling point. I couldn't take it anymore.

The feeling came on in rolling waves. A deep ache in my testicles, which felt so full and heavy, I feared they might burst. That wasn't a real thing, at least not that I'd heard of. But it felt like it.

All I knew—or believed—was that touching myself was wrong. It was the only message I'd ever received at the private Catholic school I attended.

"Don't play with your wee-wee," a nun once scolded me after walking into the bathroom to find me slapping mine around like a sausage at a urinal. I'd spent too much time in there, so she came barreling in and caught me red-handed, so to speak. I was so mortified that I never tried it again.

I was fourteen at the time. I guess you could say I was a late bloomer. The feelings intensified as I matured, going from a dull rumble to an overwhelming roar inside my body.

Eventually, I found relief in my dreams. I could never remember what I'd dreamt, but whatever it was would jostle me from my sleep. When I woke up, my underwear was stained with a wet, sticky substance I eventually learned to be semen.

The aftermath was an odd combination of deep shame and great relief. The aching was gone, but I'd wasted my seed. I was told that semen was supposed to be saved for marriage. It was only to be used for making a baby. But I couldn't help it. My body just seemed to store it up until it exploded out of me.

There were a lot of questions I had about this subject. I could never talk to my mother about them. I often wished my father was still around. Tragically, he died in a car wreck when I was ten.

Fast forward to the summer after I graduated from high school. I'd just celebrated my eighteenth birthday. Up until that time, I'd had those sticky, wet dreams once a week, two weeks at the most. But they stopped happening sometime around the first of June. Several weeks passed by and not a drop. I felt like a clogged drain.

Then one Sunday morning, the solution presented itself to me in a muscle magazine. I'd gone over to the corner drugstore by my house after morning Mass. Browsing the magazines was my usual routine on Sundays. A little bit of heaven after a little bit of hell.

I hated the doldrums of Catholic church. All that kneeling on uncomfortable benches and reciting those tiresome prayers. The only way I got through it was imagining the reward of getting a magazine after.

Oh, how I reveled in my reward too. *Adonis, Physique Pictorial, and Tomorrow's Man* were my favorite magazines. They seemed to be the standards. Each issue featured handsome young men, oiled up and flexing their muscles in skimpy bathing shorts that didn't leave much to the imagination.

I loved posing straps the most. Those tiny garments that covered the men's front business in a pouch, with spaghetti-thin straps that wrapped around their waistline, split into a 'Y' shape in the back and disappeared into the dark crevice of their round buttocks. Simply delicious.

Sometimes the men didn't wear anything at all. They'd just be casually running around by the ocean without any clothes on like a couple of knuckleheads. Or sunning themselves on the rocks by a river.

The sight of those men awakened a stirring in me. At first, I figured it was just excitement about the prospect of someday looking like them too. I'd buy the magazine, devour the pages in one sitting, and then try to burn off the energy by doing jumping jacks, push-ups, and sit-ups.

But I just couldn't seem to gain much muscle. I had a lean, tight body, not much hair. I was in good shape, but nothing like the men in the magazines.

Eventually, I realized it was more than just body envy. Not only did I aspire to look like those men someday; it was something more. I wanted to touch them, to feel their skin against mine. I wondered what they tasted like. What they smelled like. I wanted to dip my fingers inside one of those pouches and scoop up the sweat that had accumulated in the darkest, dankest regions.

Whew.

Anyway, one Sunday afternoon, I went to the drugstore after church. I was flipping through the pages, feeling this awful ache inside me, when a folded slip of paper fell out from the inner seam of the magazine. The note was hand-written:

Do you suffer from embarrassing male problems that you can't talk to your primary physician about? Come and see Dr. Doyle at 207 X Street for a free examination. Very discreet. Evenings: Friday, Saturday, and Sunday.

What a gas. I folded up the paper and stuffed it into my pocket, figuring it was someone trying to be funny.

By the twenty-fourth of June, I was desperate for relief. I'd thought about going to see our family doctor. He'd cared for me since I was born. He even went to the same church as we did. But I was afraid he'd blame me for the aching down below. Worse yet, I was afraid he'd tell my mom. So I decided to check out the address from the slip of paper.

It was a Friday night. The sun had gone down, but the darkness didn't do much to stifle the heavy heat. I rode my bicycle to X Street. The trip was uncomfortable, to say the least. The pressure of the seat crushed against my swollen walnuts.

So there I was, staring at a plain brick building on the outskirts of downtown. The area was kind of sketchy looking. Not surprising for X Street. Alphabet streets intersect with numbered streets in Sacramento. The further down the alphabet you went, the worse the area was rumored to be. I'd nearly reached the end of the line.

There wasn't even a sign over the door. Just a small white card tucked into a window: *Bathhouse & Spa Entrance, Men Only.*

That seemed kind of odd to me. I didn't know public bathhouses still existed. A vague recollection swam in my head. Something from history class involving Ancient Greece. I tried turning the doorknob, but it was locked, so I knocked.

A small cut-out popped open from the middle of the door and a man's suspicious scowl appraised me. He eyed me up and down. "Yes?"

"Um, I'm here to see the doctor." I shuffled my feet, wondering if I had the wrong place. Maybe it was a joke after all.

"The doctor?" the man asked.

I pulled the crinkled paper from my pocket and showed it to him. "Yes, I found this in a magazine."

Without confirming or denying the note, the man said, "Identification, please."

I handed him my driver's license, which he accepted through the small square. A moment later, he returned my card and said, "One nickel, please."

After handing him the coin, the door creaked open without any further discussion.

The hallway inside was dark and smelled musty, like wet towels.

"Go to the end of the hall, turn left, then right, and you'll find Dr. Doyle in the first room on your left," the man instructed. He was an older gentleman, hunched over and supporting himself with a cane.

"Left, right, then the first room on the left?" I parroted.

"That's right," the man confirmed.

"I thought you said left," I joked. My little attempt at lightening the mood.

The exasperated man sighed, not even cracking a smile. "I hope the doctor can fix you," he said ominously.

I gulped nervously, straightened my back, and headed into the shadows like a soldier marching off to war.

Left, right, left. Left, right, left...

I repeated the directions in my head, hoping the rhythm of my chant would ease my nerves.

Left, right...

The sight stopped me in my tracks. I couldn't believe what I was seeing.

An open glass-panel door led outside to a private patio area with a pool. There was a group of men gathered around it. Some were wading in the water, a few were bouncing around a striped beach ball. They were just laughing and carrying on like good pals. They looked so free and comfortable.

One of the men stood by the pool and shed a towel from around his waist, revealing a posing strap just like the ones in the magazines. His buttocks were round, firm globes. He spotted me watching and smiled.

"Don't be a peeper," he called out. "Come join us. The water feels great tonight."

"Sorry, I can't," I mumbled and then dashed away.

I came to a single doorway with two red velvet curtains hanging in front of it from floor to ceiling. A halo of light glowed around the frame of fabric.

"Ahem," I cleared my throat. "D-doctor Doyle, are you in there?"

"Please come in," a gentle voice responded.

Now was the moment of truth. I didn't understand why a doctor would be offering examinations in a bathhouse, or why he'd lure strangers with notes in muscle magazines. But I'd gotten that far, so I figured I should find out.

With my heart hammering in my ears, I reached between the curtains and spread them open.

CHAPTER 2

"Well, aren't you a sight for sore eyes," the doctor said.

There was a trace of a British accent. He was perched in an overstuffed brown leather armchair with a wooden pipe cocked to the left of his lips. A half-empty cup of tea sat beside him on a small table, next to a copy of a book titled *The City and the Pillar* and a well-worn stack of *Adonis* magazines.

The doctor was a bear of a man with raven black hair. Though he was freshly shaven his broad face seemed encased in a permanent five o'clock shadow. He wore a crisp white lab coat over a neatly ironed white button-up shirt and a maroon striped tie. His beefy thighs were casually spread open wide in traditional black slacks.

"Are you a real doctor?" I asked.

"Indeed, I am, mate. University of Liverpool, class of 1932." He thumped his chest proudly, then took a puff from his pipe.

The sweet peppery fragrance of tobacco filled the air. It conjured up a long-forgotten memory of my father, who used to smoke a pipe too. The dark, masculine aroma was long missing from my home and smelling it again made me feel oddly at ease.

"I found your note in a magazine." I held it out for him, like a small child seeking validation from an elder.

He smiled and nodded at the paper. "So what can I do for you, Mister—"

"Collins," I said. "Thomas Collins... Sir."

The doctor took the note out of my hand and set it on the table since I was just holding it there in the air, unsure what to do with it. Then he took my hand and enveloped it within his. "Nice to meet you, Mister Thomas Collins. I'm Doctor Doyle."

His touch was warm and comforting. An odd tingle rippled through me. He seemed to sense it and let go, allowing me to continue fidgeting as I stood before him awkwardly.

"So, Doctor Doyle, uh, sir, I've been having some very bad pains in my private area. Your note said you'd be discreet."

"Yes, of course, my good man. Well, tell me, when did the pains begin?"

"Around the beginning of this month."

"Can you tell me specifically where the pain is at?"

I gestured with a circle to my general groin region. "Down here."

"In your testicles?"

"Um, I guess. Well, it starts there, but it seems to spread out to my lower stomach."

The doctor rubbed his chin as he seemed to mull it over. "Tell me, have you been engaging in any type of sexual activity?"

My cheeks felt hot and I imagined I must have been as red as a strawberry. "N-n-no, of course not, sir. A nun told me that's very bad. I haven't touched myself down there in years. Honest. I mean, well... Except to go to the restroom. I have to touch myself then. Oh, and, well, to wash myself. But that's the only time I ever—"

He raised his hand to try and calm me. "Don't worry, son. I'm not here to judge you. I just want to understand your situation. Do you ever wake up in the middle of the night with something sticky in your shorts?"

How did he know about that? My heart began thudding harder; so loud I wondered if he could hear it. "Uh, yes, sir. As a matter of fact, that does happen sometimes."

"That's perfectly normal, Thomas. Your body needs to rid itself of the semen it produces. If you don't get it out manually, it will eventually release itself—usually nocturnally."

"Nocturnally?"

"When you're asleep," he explained. "Have you woken up with sticky shorts recently?"

"Well, no, sir. It used to happen every week or two, but at the start of the summer, it just seemed to stop happening."

"And that's when the pain began?"

"Mostly, yes."

He took another puff from his pipe. "What do you mean, 'mostly'?"

"I always feel kind of tight and tense, sir. Like a pot of water left on the stove to simmer. The bubbling heat is always there, like it could boil to the surface at any minute. But it never does."

"That's a colorful analogy, Thomas. Let me try and explain what's going on. These nocturnal emissions you've experienced in the past are just enough to relieve what's plugging up your pipes. Your body hasn't had a full, deep release, so you're always going to be humming along with this pent-up energy."

"But how do I get it out? I'm not married. I don't even have a girlfriend."

"Thomas, you do know what masturbation is, don't you?"

I shook my head.

"Well, you know how babies are made, don't you?"

"Of course," I said defensively.

"It's the same concept, only instead of ejaculating into a female, you just ejaculate by yourself." The doctor made a stroking motion with his hands, manipulating the air with his fingertips. "You just fondle your penis until your semen is released."

A stirring grew inside me as I began imagining a vivid scenario. "I didn't know I could do that."

The doctor chuckled. "You really have led a sheltered life, haven't you, son?"

I nodded. "Well, I can't do what you're describing, doctor. I can't touch myself."

He raised a curious eyebrow. "There are other ways to get it out."

"Without touching myself?"

"Without touching yourself," the doctor confirmed.

"How does it work?"

"I could perform a procedure rectally."

"Through my butthole?"

"It's a perfectly legitimate method," he explained. "I would begin by inserting two lubricated fingers inside you. From there, I can perform a repeated motion of massaging your vas deferens, seminal vesicle, and prostate gland. This will send a signal to your body to release the build-up."

"That sounds pretty complicated," I said.

"Anatomy sometimes is. But you have the easy part. All you have to do is relax and let me take care of the rest."

"And it won't hurt?"

"Not at all. I promise. In fact, it will feel quite pleasurable. This will allow you to experience a full and complete release."

"Doctor, I don't know. This sounds wrong. I don't think my mother would approve."

He set his pipe on the table and leaned forward, providing me a whiff of the sweet aftershave permeating from his skin. "Maybe not, Thomas. But that's the way the male anatomy was designed. These fluids must be released on a regular basis. It's part of nature. If they aren't being released nocturnally and you aren't willing to release them manually, this is the only other option I can offer."

"And you won't touch my penis?"

"I need to do a general exam of your penis and testicles, just to make sure everything is okay down there. Then I'll perform the procedure rectally. I will have complete respect for your body and will only do what is medically necessary."

"This works for other men?"

"Of course. I'm a urologist, which means I specialize in this area. Just last week, I performed this technique on a paraplegic who wanted to conceive with his wife. I successfully extracted the specimen from him by stimulating his prostate gland."

"If that's what you do for a profession, why do it here at night, in a bathhouse?"

"For men like you. You came here because you didn't feel comfortable going to a doctor's office, right?"

"Well, true," I agreed.

"It's a volunteer service I provide to help men out. Men who might not feel safe or welcome in other places. We'll take it very slowly and I'll tell you what I'm going to do before I do it. Everything will be with your consent. If you want to stop, just say so. You're free to get up and leave any time you like."

I started to feel a bit more relaxed. "Okay, let's try it."

Doctor Doyle stood up from the armchair and stretched his tree trunk arms in front of me. He was probably half a foot taller than my five-foot-nine stature. "That's a good chap. Now if you'd like to begin, let's go to my exam room and I'll get you taken care of."

CHAPTER 3

I followed the doctor into the hallway, down another corridor of this seemingly endless maze of a building. There were rows of single doors that reminded me of an apartment complex.

Some of the doors were open, revealing small rooms with a single bed and table. They were dimly lit, awash in the soft glow from a lamp. The other doors were closed and light spilled out from underneath. I could see the shadows of figures tussling. Sounds of deep moaning echoed against the walls.

A man's voice yelled out, "Yeah, that's it, buddy. Ram your big cock up my asshole. I want your cum in me."

That language. It was so obscene. I'd never heard someone speak with such vulgarity. I was titillated and terrified in the same breath.

"Is that man okay?" I asked the doctor, huddling up close to him for protection.

"Well, of course." He swung his arm around my shoulder, casually giving me a gentle squeeze. "They're relieving themselves in their own special way."

I blinked at him. "What does that mean?"

He nodded toward an open door on our left, where a man was on the bed, positioned upright on his knees, thrusting violently behind another man who was crouched in front of him. I couldn't quite see what was going on, but I could see the dominant man's bare bottom and backside glistening with sweat. His butt muscles clenched each time he propelled himself forward into the man on the receiving end.

Then all the pieces began coming together for me. They were having sexual intercourse.

"Is he..." I whispered. "Is he putting his penis in that other man's butt?"

The doctor chuckled. "Indeed, he is."

"And it feels good for them?"

"*Very.*"

"So it's sort of like what a man does to a woman?"

"Sort of."

"Does that mean I'll be girly if you put your fingers in my butt?"

We stopped in front of a door and the doctor unlocked it with a key. He put a sturdy hand on my shoulder and looked straight into my eyes.

"Thomas, all men have a prostate gland inside them, and there are thousands of nerve endings surrounding it. Those nerves provide pleasure beyond anything you can imagine. There's nothing wrong or emasculating about utilizing the gift that nature has given you. Do you understand?"

"Yes, I think so, sir."

He opened the door and gestured for me to enter. "This place is special because we don't have to worry about labels. Men can come here and do what they please. Now in your case, I want you to try and allow your mind to relax. Just focus on the way I'm going to relieve your body of all that aching that's built up."

I nodded and stepped into the room, taking stock of my surroundings. It was a double suite, like two of the rooms were combined without a wall between them. Directly in front of me was a padded exam table. To my right was a large bed that looked much more comfortable than the metal-framed ones we'd passed along the way.

"Why don't you go ahead and remove your pants and underwear, then hop up onto the table."

"Should I take off my shirt too?" It was a silly question but the words slipped out of my mouth before I could stop myself.

"Yes, please." The doctor's voice was free of judgment or criticism. He walked over to a small metal basin sink, wetted his hands, and began lathering up liberally with a bar of soap.

I chucked off my black boots, my jeans, my white Jockey underwear, and folded them neatly on a chair. Then I unbuttoned and removed my red, taupe, and white striped bowling shirt. My nervousness was made evident by the wet patches underneath the sleeves.

The doctor watched me as I climbed onto the exam table. I felt surprisingly calm under his gaze. There was something about him that put me at ease. I trusted his sparkling baby-blue eyes and the wise wrinkles that surrounded them, reflecting years of wisdom and experience.

After he'd finished washing his hands, scrubbing all the way up to his elbows, he dried off with a fresh towel and put on a pair of latex gloves.

Down the hall, I heard more voices echo their animalistic moans and groans. I began stirring inside as the doctor placed his warm hands on my back.

"Are you comfortable?" Doctor Doyle asked.

"I think so."

"It's understandable that you're a little nervous. Don't you worry, though. I'm going to take good care of you, Thomas. First, I'd like to examine your groin area. Is that alright?"

"Yes," I said with a nod.

He strolled around to the front of me and gently massaged my lower abdomen. So far, it was just like the examination I'd had with my regular doctor. But when his hand made contact with my penis, all the blood seemed to rush to the head and it sprung up like a pole.

"I'm so sorry, doctor," I apologized, covering myself.

He thoughtfully took hold of my hands and guided them away from my lap. "There's no need to apologize, Thomas. That was a perfectly normal and healthy reaction to my touching you there."

"Okay, doctor."

"May I continue examining you?"

"Yes, sir." I straightened my back and looked away, too shy to watch as his hands lifted my scrotum. He rolled each testicle between his fingers. It was a bit uncomfortable as he squeezed, but kind of exciting too.

"Everything looks good here," he confirmed. "Now I need you to lie on your side so I can begin working on your prostate."

"Okay. Which way should I face?"

"Toward the plain white wall or the plain white door. I'll be positioned behind you, so you just need to choose your view."

I chose the wall, lying on my right side and closing my eyes as he came around behind me and parted my butt cheeks. My penis was swelling, the skin pulled tight and taut because I was so painfully erect.

That's when I heard the click of something popping open, then the sound of something like liquid gel being squeezed out. As if reading my mind, the doctor began to explain.

"I'm just lubricating my fingers with K-Y jelly so they can slide in easier. Proper lubrication is essential for any type of anal penetration. It will be cold at first," he said.

A cool, slick finger brushed against the tight ring of my butthole. My whole body tensed. He waited patiently, gently massaging the rim to relax me.

It felt much better than I'd expected. I was worried it would feel like I had to go to the restroom, but as my body warmed up to his probing digit, all I felt was pleasure.

His finger dipped inside, and a strange new sensation traveled up my spine.

"You're very tight," the doctor observed.

"Oh, is that a problem?"

"Not at all. I'll just need to work you open a little more to get in my second finger."

"You're putting two fingers inside?"

"Yes. One finger will be gently manipulating your prostate gland directly. The other will be stroking up and down, which will help work out the fluids."

I didn't quite understand the logistics, but I nodded anyway.

The doctor removed his finger with a wet popping sound. Then I heard him squeezing out more gel, and felt a stronger presence knocking at my entrance.

He continued to massage my hole until he was able to work in two fingers. They were so fat and long, like two sausages prying me open. It didn't hurt. Not exactly, anyway. I just felt tension as he stretched the tight muscles of my hole.

Once he'd worked himself inside, there was a pleasing feeling of fullness. He probed me in a special spot, and the next thing I knew, a strong tingle was forcing a long string of fluid out of my throbbing penis. I gasped. "What was that? Did I just pee on myself?"

"No, it was just a little fluid from your Cowper's gland; pre-ejaculate, or pre-cum, as it's more commonly known. It was the result of my fingers connecting with your prostate gland. I can tell you're very full of semen."

He pressed again, sending more sticky fluid from my urethra. Then I felt him doing exactly what he'd described. One finger, which I presumed to be his middle, seemed to be rubbing circles around the center of that sensitive area. Then the other felt like it was gliding down a path of my inner walls, from top to bottom.

While he manipulated my insides, he firmly pressed the fingers of his left hand into the fleshy space between my butthole and my scrotum. "I'm also going to apply pressure from the outside," he explained.

The feeling began to overwhelm me as both his hands seemed to have a tight lock on my entire prostate region. My breathing became deep and shallow and my heart was pounding hard against my chest. "This is intense, doctor."

"It's okay," he whispered in a soothing voice. "Just let the feeling build. Soon, you'll get relief."

My body began to orchestrate something, a symphony I was no longer in charge of. Doctor Doyle had all the control. I lay there helplessly as waves of intense pleasure seemed to roll up and down my mid-section. I felt it all over my body, forcing me to shake.

"There you go. You're doing a great job, Thomas."

I felt possessed. Something new and strange was taking over. The hot zone radiated from behind my balls, deep inside, then traveled through the channels to every nerve receptor.

My penis was harder than it had ever been, the tip wet with fluids and flushed a deep shade of red.

"Doctor," I said breathlessly, "this is almost more than I can take."

"Shall I stop?"

The feeling had become a riptide. I was terrified, but I wanted to see where it would lead. "No, sir, please keep going."

The doctor pressed harder and more firmly, digging deep inside me like a magician reaching into his top hat. Then the strongest wave yet began building behind my aching testicles.

My penis began pulsing on its own and a boiling hot sensation surged to the surface. I could feel it rising to the very top of my glans. Then a river of thick, white fluid exploded out.

It shot nearly a foot in front of me, splattering against the wall. And the pulsing continued, flinging another rope of pearl liquid out, which landed on the floor.

The doctor kept a firm grip on my prostate gland, pushing out more and more semen until it slowed to a leak. Finally, he released his grip, slowly pulling out his two fingers.

I felt twenty pounds lighter, like a heavy pressure had finally left my body. The doctor looked down at me with a satisfied smile as I rolled over onto my back, panting like an animal.

"You're finally free," he said.

And I was.

CHAPTER 4

The feeling of euphoria stayed with me all the way home, where I crawled into bed with a big, dopey grin on my face and drifted off to sleep in the clouds.

But the next morning, I awoke with a massive erection that tented up from my bedsheets. My whole body seemed to crackle with electricity. My skin was sensitive all over. Even the gentle pressure of my cotton Jockeys against my swollen wood was too much for me to handle.

I threw on a robe and hurried out into the hallway, where I barely missed slamming into my sister with my sword. What an embarrassment that would have been. She scowled at me as she left the bathroom, drying her freshly washed hair with a towel.

That's what I needed. A good, cold shower to calm me down.

But the water was lukewarm. That damn Sacramento summer heat kept the pipes warm, even at the start of the day. So I only turned on the right knob, trying to keep it as cold as possible. The cascading sensation of water on my cock did nothing but drive me crazy.

My cock.

I'd never called it that before, not even to myself.

That's what that man in the spa had called it. "*Ram your big cock up my asshole*," I heard him say.

Cock. The word only seemed to excite me more. It seemed the lukewarm shower wasn't going to do anything to help me, so I turned the water off and grabbed a towel.

What next? I wondered. The doctor had relieved my ache, but it only made me want more.

And then...

My head was racing with possibilities. If a doctor could bring me that much satisfaction with only his fingers, I wondered what it would feel like to have a penis inside me. No, not a penis. *A cock.*

What would it feel like to have a man's hard cock in there, hot to the touch, pulsing with veins and filling me with his semen?

Er, wait. *Cum.* That's what the man called it. What would that feel like?

For every question I had, there were five more questions to follow, and none with any answers. Those thoughts had to be wrong. It was one thing for the doctor to help me with a medical procedure, I rationalized. But actually engaging with other men; that would be very wrong.

I started thinking about all those men playing in the pool. It was a scene more magical than I could have ever dreamt of. Like one of my muscle magazines come to life. A safe place where men could be with men the same way they were with women.

Those men looked so happy. Frolicking around the pool in their posing straps. Frolicking wasn't wrong. Just guys being guys.

The bathhouse was a *special* place, as the doctor had described it.

But it was the other stuff. The men paired together, sullying the sheets of those creaky beds. Thrashing about like wild animals.

Oh, god.

I threw on some clothes and coasted through the kitchen, grabbing a piece of toast from the table where my mother and sister ate breakfast.

"Where are you off to?" my mother asked. She wasn't usually the curious type, but that day, of all days, she just had to ask.

"Oh, I need to run a few errands. Say, ma, is it alright if I borrow your car?"

She eyed me with skepticism. "I suppose. Just be home for lunch."

"Thanks," I said, giving her a peck on the cheek and then dashing out the back kitchen door before she could ask more questions.

There was a sports shop on the other side of town that sold all kinds of gear and uniforms. I was never big on sports, so I only shopped there when I needed a new pair of clothes for gym class. But they had everything there, so it was the best place I could think of.

I walked into the store feeling like a stranger in a foreign land. A man at the sales counter nodded to me.

"Good morning," he said. We were the only two in there. I could see he was in the middle of reading the newspaper so I hoped that would keep him occupied while I browsed.

"Morning," I said, avoiding his eyes.

"Anything I can help you find?"

"No, thank you. I'm just looking." The main floor was crammed full of free-standing racks lined in uneven rows. Each aisle was stuffed with clothing that hung from mismatched hangers.

"Okay, then." He took a sip from his coffee mug and went back to his reading. Probably the sports section.

Baseball uniforms, running shorts, protective padding...

Nope, nope, nope...

As I skimmed row after row, inching further and further from the prying eyes of the salesman, I finally spotted what I was hoping to find in the far left corner, tucked away by some exercise equipment on the wall.

There, on a small rack, was a display of posing straps. I ran my hands along the soft cotton fabric, laced my fingers through the barely-there bands.

"We just started selling those. Are you a model or something?" the man asked. I turned to find him watching me again. He'd lit a cigarette and smoke billowed from his nostrils.

"No."

"Some sort of swimmer?"

I shook my head as I thumbed through the colors. White, black, or red. Those were my options.

The man behind the counter persisted. "Well, what would you wear those for?"

Ignoring his question, I asked, "What size are these?

"They're supposed to be one size fits all. The strap is adjustable."

I snatched a white pouch off the rack, hoping it would fit my slender body the way I imagined, and took it up to the counter.

He didn't ask any more questions as he punched the numbers into the register.

$3.99

I could have bought a whole pack of my Jockey shorts for that. But this was going to be worth it. I hurried out of the store, anxious to get home and try on my new purchase.

CHAPTER 5

The rough denim of my jeans seemed to rake against my skin with every move I made that day. I walked around wearing my new posing strap underneath my pants and felt alive with sexual energy. Completing my chores around the house was a slow form of torture for me. Bending over to pick something up caused the thin strap to tighten between my legs, brushing gently against my butthole.

I reacted with a shudder, remembering the way it felt when the doctor's thick fingers were prying me open. I wanted to feel him there again, massaging my throbbing insides until he coaxed a satisfying release that would take me to a dream-like state of bliss.

Every minute and every hour of the day passed slowly. I just needed to make it until dark. That's when I'd be free to go back to that sacred place. It was a Saturday night. I was desperately hoping he'd be there, just as his hand-written note had stated. *Evenings: Friday, Saturday, and Sunday.* I'd need to get a summer job just to pay for all the trips I planned to make to see him. Maybe get a bus pass too.

Would three times a week be enough? I wondered if I could start visiting him at his office too.

My fever was spreading. I needed his special touch so badly.

I waited until seven-thirty that evening. It wasn't dark yet but the sun was setting and I figured I could get into the building without seeing anyone I knew. The location was pretty discreet anyway.

Every bump of the bicycle ride caused sweet agony. The friction was driving me mad. When I arrived, the man at the front door regarded me with a wry smile that made me feel a little ashamed for coming back.

"The doctor didn't cure you?" he asked smugly through the small cut-out in the door.

I felt like a gluttonous pig, going back to the trough for another helping. What if there was no cure? What if the more times it happened, the hungrier I'd be? These were the sinful indulgences I'd been warned about.

While fishing some change out of my pants, I dropped some coins on the concrete and bent over to collect them. Again, the strap flicked at my hole, and I knew there was no turning back.

I handed my nickel through the door without providing a response. The man didn't need to know why I was there. It was none of his concern.

He let me inside, smiled widely, and said, "Have fun."

Something was in the air that night. I could smell it. In fact, I could probably have cut it with a knife. This heady combination of bleach and sweat and something else. Pure, raw sexuality, I suppose.

I made my lap down the halls and around the corners, knowing my way around like a regular patron. When I passed the outside patio area, I slowed down my gait, allowing myself to linger a little longer. Quite a few more men were in the water that evening. Most of them wore shorts, but a few of them, the really muscular ones, were strutting around in only their posing straps. I felt like I belonged, wearing my own white pouch underneath. One of the guys turned to me and winked. Surprisingly, I winked back.

When I got to that same familiar velvet curtain, the smell of the doctor's tobacco pipe wafted into my nostrils. I felt like I'd made my way home.

"Doctor, are you in there?" I asked.

The head of a young man poked out. "The doctor's not here."

The young man's hair was reddish-brown and slicked back in a pompadour style. He had green eyes and freckles on pale skin.

"Oh, um..." I looked down at my shoes, trying to avoid the young man's sparkling gaze. He had to be my age, or maybe a year or two older, but I didn't recognize him from school. "Well, do you know when he'll be back?"

The young man shook his head. "No, but I was waiting for him too."

"Oh."

"You can come in here and join me... If you want," the man offered.

"Okay." I stepped inside to find him standing in a black posing strap. The blood rushed to my cock and I was instantly hard. His body was lean and muscular, much more defined than mine, especially around his firm chest and round shoulders. He must have been involved in some type of sport that builds upper body strength. Swimming, maybe, or baseball, I guessed.

He blushed and folded his arms across his chest modestly. "Sorry, I was already undressed."

"That's okay. I like your, uh..." I pointed toward his pouch, which was stuffed full. He must have been a big guy. "Garment."

"Thanks. I just bought it this afternoon. The man at the store gave me a funny look and made a crack about how the pouches were becoming so popular."

I chuckled. "That's probably because I went in there this morning and bought one too."

"Oh, makes sense." He surveyed my body, then asked, "Can I see yours?"

I hesitated but figured it was only fair, so I unzipped my jeans and let them fall down to my ankles.

"Ah, you bought the white one," he observed, as if it revealed some deep secret about me.

"Yeah, that's the kind I see in a lot of magazines. You can't go wrong with white."

"The color of purity," he said with a sly grin. "It looks really good on you."

I couldn't help but blush. "Thank you. Yours looks good on you too."

"Can I feel it?"

My breath caught in my throat. He was so brazen. He just asked for what he wanted. His confidence got me even more excited. "Uh, sure."

He extended his lithe fingers toward my pouch and hooked them in from the side straps, stroking down against my skin mere centimeters from my raging erection.

"Mind if I feel yours too?" I asked.

He nodded. "Go ahead and touch it."

I reached out and rubbed the line of his fabric, feeling its smooth texture against my fingertips. I could sense the heat emanating from his body.

"Do you come here often?" I asked.

"I see the doctor once a week."

"That frequently, huh?"

The young man nodded. "He's the best."

"And he really is a doctor?" I couldn't help myself from asking. I already knew it was true. He was so good at what he did, I just couldn't believe he'd help guys out for free during his spare time.

"Yep, a urologist," the young man confirmed. "When he's here, he's not acting in his official capacity, of course. He could lose his license. But he uses his skill and experience to help fellas out."

"Interesting."

"Sorry to keep you chaps waiting," a deep voice said.

We both pulled away from each other and tried to look casual, like two kids who'd been caught with their hands in the cookie jar.

Doctor Doyle stood in the doorway, looking charming in his crisp white lab coat. "I see you two have already gotten acquainted."

"Not formally," the young man said, extending his hand to me. "Bobby Rogers."

"Thomas Collins," I said, giving his hand a squeeze. "Nice to meet you."

The doctor eyed us both with his kind baby blues. "So, who's first?"

I nodded toward Bobby. "He was here before I was. I can wait outside."

"Well, actually," Bobby said, "I was wondering if Thomas could stay and watch."

That earned a genuine smile from the handsome doctor, which made my heart flutter.

"I'm fine with that," Doctor Doyle confirmed. "Thomas, would you like to watch?"

I looked at both men nervously as they exchanged glances. A secret conversation was being had, spoken with their eyes in a language only they could understand.

"W-w-what, uh, what exactly would I be watching?" I stammered over my words.

"Remember what you witnessed last night in those rooms?" the doctor asked.

I gulped. "Yes, sir."

The doctor smiled broadly.

I couldn't help smiling back, feeling warm all over. "I think I get the picture."

"Bobby and I are going to head over to the exam room. If you'd like to watch, you can. If not, please wait here and I'll tend to you in a bit." The doctor turned and walked out before I could respond, and Bobby followed after. I only hesitated for a split-second, then frantically pulled my pants back up and followed right behind them.

We passed through the hallway of rowdy guests. The sound of their moans and groans was music to me. When we arrived in the exam room, Bobby already seemed to know his place. He climbed on top of the exam table and kneeled on his hands and knees.

Sliding his pouch down to his knees, a long crystal string of fluid broke away from the head of his hardened cock. He'd made a sticky mess inside his underwear.

"So, as I was saying," the doctor explained, "what you saw yesterday..."

"Yes, sir," I said with a nod.

"That's what I do to Bobby every Saturday night."

"Oh," I said dumbly. "I didn't know that was a medical procedure too."

The doctor chuckled softly. "Doctors like to have fun too, Thomas. Sometimes men come to me with embarrassing problems and I give them advice. They don't even take their clothes off. And sometimes, in cases like yours, they just need a helping hand—or finger." He raised a playful eyebrow. "And sometimes, we take things a little further. What Bobby and I have is special. Every Saturday night, he visits me and I take care of his needs."

"We take care of each other's needs," Bobby amended with a grin.

Doctor Doyle smiled and kissed Bobby gently on the shoulder, then caressed his lean bicep.

Just seeing them together made my cock stir. They were both so handsome to me in different ways. Bobby, being the young, toned fella with a rock-solid body. And Doctor Doyle, being older, wiser, with his glinting eyes and his voice filled with authority. There was such a contrast between them and I couldn't believe I was really going to witness their intimacy up close and personal.

The doctor gestured to a lonely plastic chair pushed against the wall. "If you'd like to stay, please make yourself comfortable and have a seat."

I followed his directions and sat in the chair. The show began to unfold in front of me as Doctor Doyle continued caressing Bobby's body with his big hands. He kissed the back of Bobby's neck and traced a trail down his spine, all the way to the crest of his buttocks. Judging by the soft moans that escaped Bobby's lips, he seemed to be enjoying it.

Then the doctor's thick tongue darted out, stiff and pointed on the end, licking a path between Bobby's butt cheeks as he spread them apart. Bobby's moans grew louder and the doctor seemed to relish in the taste.

I wondered what it was like to be licked down there. The thought had never even crossed my mind, but now I couldn't help feeling a little bit jealous. I wanted the doctor's mouth on me, tasting me and giving me the same attention.

But instead, I decided to wait it out. I just wanted to observe, like an audience member sitting in a movie theater. Everything was happening on the big screen in front of me, but I was still at a safe distance. It didn't feel real to me yet.

As the doctor leaned over the table, licking, nibbling, and teasing Bobby's hole, he shrugged off his white lab coat to reveal a large tent in his black slacks. It looked like he was smuggling a small person down there. *His cock must be massive,* I thought.

Off came the doctor's shirt, revealing a dense forest of dark chest hair. He was a solid brute encased by a sheet of muscle. I knew he was burly but hadn't expected him to be so built under his clothes. Quite a difference next to Bobby's lean and mostly bare athletic build.

The moment of truth came as the doctor unfastened his pants and let them fall to the floor. With his face still buried between Bobby's cheeks, he pulled down his blue and white striped boxer shorts, and the beast was unleashed.

Nestled in a thick bush of curls, the doctor's cock stood large and stiff. Protruding from his veiny foreskin was a meaty helmet head that glistened in the light. It looked like smooth marble. I found my mouth watering as I imagined tasting it.

"You ready for me to take your temperature, boy?" Doctor Doyle said in a husky growl, slapping Bobby's bottom playfully.

"Yes, doctor."

The doctor grabbed a tube of K-Y from a nearby table. "What are your symptoms?" he asked.

"I feel hot all over."

"Uh-huh," the doctor grunted as he palmed a glob of jelly across his cock head. "What else?"

"I have an itch I can't scratch."

"Oh, yeah? Where?"

Bobby reached behind and tapped his butthole. "Right inside there. Really deep."

The doctor dipped his middle finger inside Bobby and hooked it downward. "Right there?"

Bobby bit his lower lip and nodded.

"I've got just the cure for that." The doctor took his large cock into his hand and pressed it against Bobby's hole, sinking forward slowly as the young man's body opened up to him.

I watched in astonishment, wondering how something so big could fit inside such a tight little body. But Bobby seemed to take it like a pro. He moaned with pleasure as the doctor effortlessly glided deep into his hole.

With their bodies connected, they moved in rhythm together. When the doctor pulled out, Bobby pushed back. Then they both gasped as they crashed together again.

In and out.

Over and over.

My own cock was raging hard and there was a deep stirring inside me. I began to realize that a tickle from the doctor's fingers wasn't going to be enough to satiate me. Not after seeing this. I wanted more. I wanted what they had.

That carnal connection. A shared understanding of each other's needs. Two bodies melting together. I wanted to feel it too. Hot skin against skin, a hard organ thrusting its way inside me.

This was human nature, and in that moment, the shame and embarrassment for the feelings I'd kept locked away seemed to dissipate. It was only instinct at work.

Without really thinking about what I was doing, my fingers found their way to my shirt and lifted it over my head. The fabric was too constricting. My body needed to breathe. Then my fingers found their way to the top button of my jeans. I popped it open, then down came the teeth of my zipper, which was scraping mercilessly against my throbbing cock.

Even my posing strap was too tight against me. Down it went too. Then I was sitting there with my bare butt cheeks pressed against the rickety chair watching the magic happen.

Doctor Doyle was really giving it to Bobby good; thrusting hard and deep into him, jaw clenched and muscles flexed as he held the boy steady by the hips with his big hands. Their rhythm was faster now, more fervent. Bobby had reached between his legs and begun stroking his cock. The look on their faces told me they were close to reaching the finish line together.

Meanwhile, my cock was swollen and dripping with pre-cum. I wasn't ready for the show to be over yet. Not yet.

I wasn't myself anymore. As if possessed by a bolder, braver incarnation of my spirit, I yelled out, "Stop!"

CHAPTER 6

They both looked at me with bewilderment. "I think our friend Thomas has something to tell us," the doctor said wryly.

"Yes," I said, licking my lips. "I want to be part of that."

Bobby and the doctor looked at each other, grinning as they once again seemed to speak a secret language with their eyes.

Then Bobby tossed his head to the side as if to say, 'Come on over here.'

I chucked off the rest of my clothes as I sauntered over to them.

First, I wanted to taste Bobby's cock, so I sank to my knees and opened my mouth to receive him. He smeared the underside of his shaft against my wanting tongue and squeezed from the base, pushing out a long rope of pre-cum.

I licked it clean, tasting the subtle saltiness, then wrapped my lips around the head and carefully took his cock into my mouth. I'd never done that before, so I wasn't quite sure how to suck it, but I knew enough to avoid using my teeth. By the sound Bobby made, I seemed to be doing an alright job.

It felt good to have his hot, hard cock in my mouth. He was being very patient too, letting me be the driver and swallow him at my own pace. I managed to get most of the length down until it hit the back of my throat. Then I gagged and momentarily panicked as my air supply was cut off.

"Take your time," Bobby said, caressing my hair and smoothing it to the side.

"Let me help you relax," the doctor said. He'd pulled out of Bobby's hole and was now spread out sideways on the floor, supporting himself on his left elbow while he used his right hand to take my cock into his mouth.

The feeling was like instant fireworks as the doctor devoured my cock effortlessly. He worked the head with his tongue, kissing and slurping it, then swallowed me down until his nose was buried in my pubes.

It was so damn incredible.

I returned my attention to Bobby's cock, trying to balance the task of learning how to suck him off while also enjoying the intense ecstasy I felt at the doctor's skilled service.

My throat muscles seemed to be more receptive to the foreign visitor because Bobby's cock slid down my throat until I'd taken him to the base. He let out a loud moan that grew from his belly as I took all of him inside me. I was choking on his cock, but I closed my eyes and focused on breathing through my nose.

"That's it," he said, pulling at my hair. "Take that cock."

His sexy dirty talk turned me on even more and I felt a strand of pre-cum leak from the slit of my own cock. The doctor was busy giving my nut sack a tongue bath, but he quickly moved up to catch the drip, licking me clean.

My orgasm was rolling to the surface and I wasn't sure I could last much longer. I pulled away from Bobby's cock to free my mouth, and said, "Doctor, you're about to make me come."

There was a bridge of saliva between his juicy, smiling pink lips and my overly sensitive glans. "Good," he whispered. "That's the goal."

"But I want to do so much more."

He smiled confidently. "And you will. There are plenty of opportunities ahead of you, son. What would you like to try now?"

I looked up at Bobby. "Well..." I hesitated as a scene came alive in my head.

Standing up, I instructed Bobby to get in front of me and the doctor to get behind me. This business of being in charge wasn't so bad. I kind of liked it.

I grabbed the tube of jelly and squeezed out a generous amount, which I worked all over my cock head and down the shaft. Then I squeezed out more and rubbed it onto the doctor's cock. He was so thick and hard in my hand. I could only pray he wouldn't break me.

"Okay," I said, pressing my bottom into the doctor's lap. "First, I want you to break the seal."

The doctor chuckled. "*Break the seal?* I love it."

I grit my teeth as he began leaning into my virgin hole. He was slow and steady, giving my body time to warm up to his thick flared head. The first threshold only felt like a minor sting. He stopped and instructed me to breathe. I let my chest rise and fall with full inhales and exhales.

Doctor Doyle pushed deeper, and I felt the ring of my hole tighten and spasm in protest. It was like he was driving a truck inside me.

"Just keep breathing," the doctor said, placing a warm hand on my shoulder. I instantly felt soothed by his touch.

I pushed back further while he pressed forward. The inner walls of my hole massaged his slick cock, expanding open to take his girth.

"That's my boy," he whispered. "Just like that."

It hurt and felt good, all at once. My body was bucking at the new and unfamiliar feeling.

The doctor pulled back out slowly, always acting with care, and slathered another thick coat of jelly onto his cock. Then he leaned into me again. This time he seemed to glide in with much less resistance.

"Ah, that's good," I said with a satisfied sigh.

"Son, that's just the head," the doctor said.

"What?" I looked over my shoulder to see him grinning at me.

"Why don't you just focus on Bobby? That will help loosen up your muscles."

I turned to Bobby and cupped his firm glutes. They were so taut in my hands. "You ready, Bobby?"

"Give it all to me," he said, looking over his shoulder with a glimmer in his eyes.

He leaned back against me while I pressed my cock into him. His hole was warm and pliable, swallowing me down without resistance. It felt like my entire cock was enveloped in a warm, wet hug. Pure heaven.

So this is what all the fuss is about, I thought.

The sheen of sweat glistened on Bobby's skin. I breathed into the back of his neck, then kissed it. I don't know why I was kissing someone I'd just met. It just felt right.

I tasted the salt of his skin. He shivered as goosebumps formed over the surface. I gently rolled my tongue down the middle of his back while we gyrated our hips together. My cock probed in and out of his glorious hole, sending tingling waves that swam to my balls.

Not to be outdone or forgotten, Doctor Doyle began thrusting deeper into me. My inner walls burned as his massive beast of a cock pried me open. But pleasure outpaced the pain and soon the entire lower trunk of my body was swallowed up by ecstasy. From my front to my back and everywhere in between, I was buzzing with amazing feelings I'd never known before.

"Are you okay, mate?" the doctor's deep voice vibrated into my ear.

I was so breathless, I could hardly speak. "Yes, but I—"

The warmth of his thick, hairy forearms wrapped around me and then he squeezed my nipples between his fingertips. That sent another wave straight down my core.

"I don't know if I can handle it," I murmured. "I don't know who to focus on and I don't want to finish too quickly."

Every time I rocked my hips forward, I buried myself to the root of my shaft inside Bobby while riding up the pole of Doctor Doyle. Then when I leaned back, Bobby's tight hole clamped greedily onto my cock head, as if desperate to keep hold of me while my hungry hole went down on the doctor.

"You're overthinking it," the doctor said. "Picture a dam being pummeled by a rushing river of water. It's filling to the top, spilling over the edges, and you're trying so hard to keep it contained. Let it break free. You're safe here. You won't drown in your feelings."

He was right. I closed my eyes and immersed myself in the pleasure. The two men began tag-teaming me so I wouldn't have to do any work. Bobby was impaling himself on my cock, riding up and down on my swollen rod while the doctor grabbed hold of my hips and began pounding me fast and hard.

Heat bloomed from somewhere deep inside me. My prostate gland, I realized. It was the same build-up I'd had the night before. I began quivering all over. Then something else began stirring inside my balls and climbing up to the head of my cock. It was like two types of orgasms surging together.

Sweat dripped from our bodies as we crashed into one another. Then I heard a loud, guttural scream tear through the air. It was just like the scream I'd heard when I saw that man bent over getting fucked on the bed. The man who sounded like he was getting murdered.

That's when I realized the screaming was coming from me. I'd never yelled out in such a primal way before. It seemed to erupt from my lungs without my control. My throat opened up and all my ghosts of repression were set free.

Then my whole body shook, my muscles tensed and tightened. "Ahhh, yeaaah!" I shouted out as I shot a wad of cum deep inside Bobby. My spirit felt lifted. I'd ascended from earth. And the river I'd held back came flooding out of me.

Doctor Doyle started growling like an animal, wild and untamed. He clutched my hips tighter and dug his fingers into my flesh. I could feel his gigantic cock stiffen and the bulbous head swelled, then he bucked as he dumped his fiery load of cum inside me.

Both my virgin cock and virgin hole had been thoroughly tended to that night. I felt like a new man. The inhibited Thomas Collins was gone for good. But I wasn't done yet.

Bobby had resumed pumping his cock while riding mine. I was still hard as a rock too, though my cock was feeling overly sensitive post-orgasm.

"Wait a minute," I said, taking hold of Bobby's right hand. "I want to finish what I started earlier."

I pulled apart from Bobby while Doctor Doyle
dismounted from my sloppy, wet hole. I immediately missed
the girthy feeling of fullness inside me.

"Where do you want me?" Bobby asked.

I spun him around on the exam table so he could face me.
"You're fine where you are." His underwear was down at his
ankles. I pulled it off and examined the sticky mess smeared
inside the pouch. Taking a deep inhale, I enjoyed the dank
aroma of his ball sweat mixed with pre-cum.

"Why stand there and sniff my dirty underwear when you
can enjoy it fresh from the source?" Bobby said.

I grinned and knelt down between his legs, devouring his
earthy scent. He'd been fresh and clean at the start of the night.
Right out of the shower. But now the smells of sex and
testosterone emanated from him.

I didn't mind. With my open mouth and thirsty tongue, I
began lapping the sweat from his low-hanging nut sack and
then licked away the gooey clear fluid that was all over his
cock.

Then I traced a path up the treasure trail of hair that led to
his naval, worked up to his perky nipples, and settled into the
curls under his armpits.

Bobby was a fountain of sex. Everything that flowed from
him smelled and tasted delicious. I didn't even mind the biting
tartness of his pit sweat. I would eat him on a platter.

Doctor Doyle got down on the floor underneath me and
began flicking his tongue around my hole while I serviced

Bobby. I was still loose and spread open from his pounding, so his forceful tongue pushed right inside me. It felt wonderful being fucked with the rigid tip.

I took Bobby into my mouth and began licking circles around his cock head while stroking his shaft with my hand. He started moaning loudly, letting me know he was already on the edge.

"That's it," he whispered through labored breaths. He gripped a fist-full of my hair and pulled so hard I thought my follicles were being ripped from my scalp. I didn't let the burning pain slow me down. It just made me work with more zeal, sucking and slurping his spit-soaked cock.

Without another utterance of warning, his glans swelled and his slit burst open to fill my mouth with the first explosive shot of cum. I'd never tasted semen before. The flavor was salty and tangy with a thick, oily consistency. It was scolding hot and heavy as it coated the back of my throat. I gulped down every drop, twirling my tongue around the head to coax out any dribble I could get.

More! I needed more! I reveled in the bleachy aftertaste of Bobby's cum.

Doctor Doyle sat up from between my butt cheeks. "Let's trade," he said.

His lips parted and his mouth settled on mine. He slid his tongue inside and deposited a glob of semen. That's when I realized what he'd been doing when he was sucking on my battered hole like a vacuum cleaner. He'd scooped his own load out of my hole.

Our tongues danced. I shared what was left of Bobby's release and let the flavors mingle with the doctor's offering. When I swallowed, I felt happy having them both inside me. Down my throat. In my hole. I could still smell the sweat of Bobby's nut sack and armpits smeared all over my face.

Bobby hopped down from the exam table and we settled into a sticky pile on the floor. In the middle was Doctor Doyle, who extended his strong arms around both of us and pulled us tight against his wooly pecs.

"Are you satisfied?" he asked me.

I smiled through heavy eyelids. In the afterglow of our threesome, I felt relaxed and content. "For now."

The doctor ruffled my hair. "I knew you'd be a hungry one. I could tell it as soon as you wandered your tight little bottom in here yesterday."

"But I was so shy."

"You just didn't know yourself yet," he explained.

He was right. I would never go back to the wound-tight shy guy I'd been my whole life. I was a grown man. Eighteen-years-old. A high school graduate. My future was up to me. Once I knew there were other men out there like me, who existed beyond the pages of those muscle physique magazines, I felt like I was standing in front of a buffet. I wanted to try every dish on the menu.

"What would you guys think of some more group activities?" I asked.

Doctor Doyle smiled over at me. "I think you boys should go off and explore on your own."

I blinked with surprise.

Bobby explained, "The doctor prefers spending his free time helping guys. He derives more pleasure from taking care of them than having himself taken care of. He doesn't do this with just anyone."

"Oh, of course," I said, feeling silly for asking.

The doctor cradled my face in his large hands. "Don't you go feeling bad now, mate. I'm proud of you for getting in touch with your true desires. You've grown so much these past two nights. Bobby here came to me just a few months ago with the same problems you had."

Turning to Bobby with wide eyes, I said, "You did?"

Bobby nodded. "It took me a while to get comfortable, but now here I am having a three-way."

Doctor Doyle squeezed us both in a bear hug. "I want you boys to go out there, be young, and have fun. I'm going to take a quick shower, then return to my little makeshift office to see who else needs my help. There's probably a line down the hallway by now."

My fingers danced across Doctor Doyle's broad chest, playing in the meadow of dark hair. "Well, sir, Bobby and I need to take a shower too. Maybe the three of us could lather up together."

Bobby and the doctor glanced at each other. It was one of those knowing exchanges again. But this time, I felt like I spoke their language too.

"Okay, boys, I guess my patients can wait another ten minutes," Doctor Doyle said. "Let's hit the showers."

We stood and I grabbed a towel from a fresh stack of laundry. I whipped it against Bobby's bare bottom, where it landed with a loud crack. He laughed and took off running. I chased after him.

The doctor strutted close behind, having no trouble scooping me up and slinging me over his shoulder. His hot, sweaty skin clung to mine as I bounced around eyeing his meaty butt. I took a firm mound in my hand and squeezed, deciding that would be the next cave I'd conquer. As soon as we got to the showers, I planned to dive into that moist terrain and explore it. His patients were going to be waiting a little longer.

That night was just the beginning of the best summer of my life.

ALSO AVAILABLE FROM NATHAN BAY

King of the Sea

The Invisible Plan

Young Forever

Bathhouse Confessions

Visit amazon.com/author/nathanbay for news + info.

Made in the USA
Coppell, TX
23 October 2021